Terrible Times

Over two metres tall, with a bushy beard, Philip Ardagh is not only very large and very hairy – and revered as a god in some of the less well explored areas of Camberwell – but has also written over fifty children's books for all ages. *Terrible Times* is the third book in the bestselling Eddie Dickens trilogy, which began with *Awful End* and *Dreadful Acts*, both of which were shortlisted for book awards.

Currently living as a full-time writer, with a wife and two cats in a seaside town somewhere in England, he has been – amongst other things – an advertising copywriter, a hospital cleaner, a (highly unqualified) librarian, and a reader for the blind.

by the same author
published by Faber & Faber

Fiction

The Eddie Dickens Trilogy
Awful End
Dreadful Acts

The Further Adventures of Eddie Dickens
Dubious Deeds

Unlikely Exploits
The Fall of Fergal
Heir of Mystery

Non-fiction

The Hieroglyphs Handbook
Teach Yourself Ancient Egyptian

The Archaeologist's Handbook
The Insider's Guide to Digging Up the Past

Did Dinosaurs Snore?
$100^1/_2$ Questions about Dinosaurs Answered

Why Are Castles Castle-Shaped?
$100^1/_2$ Questions about Castles Answered

Philip Ardagh

TERRIBLE TIMES

Book Three of the Eddie Dickens Trilogy

illustrated by David Roberts

faber and faber

First published in 2002
by Faber and Faber Limited
3 Queen Square, London WC1N 3AU
This paperback edition first published in 2003

Typeset by Faber and Faber Limited
Printed in England by Mackays of Chatham plc, Chatham, Kent

© Philip Ardagh, 2002
Illustrations © David Roberts, 2002

Philip Ardagh is hereby identified as author of this work in accordance
with Section 77 of the Copyright, Designs and Patents Act 1988

A CIP record for this book
is available from the British Library

ISBN 0-571-21622-6

2 4 6 8 10 9 7 5 3 1

For Suzy Jenvey and Vivian French

A Message from the Author

Whose beard is now out of control

If this is the first Eddie Dickens book you've come across, DON'T PANIC!!! Each book is a self-contained adventure. For those of you who have come with me and Eddie all the way from *Awful End* to here, though, I hope you've enjoyed the ride. A number of readers – okay, a *lot* of readers – have asked why this is the last Eddie Dickens book and why I'm not going to write any more. The last Eddie Dickens book? Says who? This may be the last of the trilogy, but what's to stop me writing some 'further adventures' some day? You know, I get the feeling I might just do that. In the meantime, I hope you enjoy *Terrible Times*.

PHILIP ARDAGH
England
2002

Contents

Episode 1

Explosive News!

In which America is mentioned, but the author gets somewhat side-tracked

'America?' said Eddie Dickens in amazement. 'You want me to go to America?' His mother nodded. This was difficult because she was wearing an enormous neck brace, which looked rather like one of those huge plastic collars vets sometimes put around dogs' heads, to prevent them from licking wounds; only hers was made of whalebone and starched linen.

Before you start crying 'Poor whale!' and writing off letters of complaint, I wish to point out two things: firstly, these events took place in the

1

19th century when things were very different to the 21st; secondly, the whale whose bones were used to make the frame for Mrs Dickens's neck brace had died of natural causes after a long and fulfilling life at sea, with plenty of singing which is, apparently, what whales like doing most.

Okay, it hadn't said, 'When I die, I hope my bones are used to make surgical appliances,' but it's better than being harpooned and killed in its prime in order to make surgical appliances. (I say 'it' simply because I don't know whether this particular whale was a he or a she. Sorry.)

Not that Eddie or his mother were thinking of such matters, as they walked up the drive of Awful End, that cold winter's afternoon. She'd just dropped the bombshell about wanting Eddie to go to America. I don't mean she'd *actually* dropped a bombshell, of course. Not a real one. That's simply an expression for a surprising piece of news. She did drop a real bombshell once, funnily enough – actually it was a mortar shell, but it was packed with explosives like a bomb and did go off which explains why she was now wearing the neck brace and, oh yes, walked with the aid of crutches.

She was lucky not to have been more seriously injured. Fortunately for her, when she'd tripped and stumbled with the shell – it was like a big brass tube, or a giant bullet, not something a hermit crab lives in on the beach – she'd tossed it over a small wall, dividing the rose garden from the sunken garden. It was the sunken garden which took much of the blast, but it wasn't badly damaged either. A lot of earth flew all over the place and an ornamental pear tree was destroyed, but little else. Less fortunately, one of Mad Uncle Jack's ex-soldier colleagues (who'd been sleeping under the rhubarb, which afforded great shade under its huge leaves) was blown to smithereens (which isn't a small seaside town near Bridlington, but means 'to bits'). Eddie's mum was horrified. She felt guilty for days, and never ate rhubarb again for the rest of her life, except in crumbles or with custard . . . or a light sprinkling of brown sugar. Or white, if there was no brown.

Mad Uncle Jack tried to reassure her by saying that, if the chap had been a half-decent soldier, he would have been heroically blown up in some battle long ago. And, anyway, he strongly suspected that the fool had been chewing the rhubarb leaves, which are highly poisonous, so he'd probably have been dead by now whether she'd tripped and tossed the shell over the wall or not.

Before we get back to Eddie and Mrs Dickens crunching up the drive to Awful End, and her telling her son about the plans for America, there may be those amongst you who are interested to know why Mrs Dickens was carrying the shell in the first place. Quite simply, it was because she'd found it in her sewing box. It was summertime (you might have guessed that from the size of the rhubarb leaves) and she was fed up with the early morning light coming through the crack between the curtains, so she'd decided to sew them together. Instead of finding her usual rows of cotton reels, little pot of pins, her packet of needles, and dried broad beans (graded by size) she found the brass mortar shell and nothing else.

Puzzled, she'd gone in search of her husband, Mr Dickens, whom she knew was painting the garden.

Mr Dickens wasn't painting the garden in the sense that John Constable might paint a landscape or Turner a seascape, with oil paints on to a canvas. No, Mr Dickens was going around the garden painting some of the leaves a greener green. As he was getting older – and he wasn't *that* old – his eyesight wasn't quite what it had been, and some colours (especially browns and greens) seemed duller, which was why he was going around with a pot of bright green paint and a badger-bristle paintbrush. Unfortunately, unlike the whale, I've no idea whether this particular badger died of natural causes. I'm very, very, sorry.

Having found the shell in her otherwise empty sewing box and knowing her husband was painting the trees, the garden was a logical place for Eddie's mother to go, and how she came to drop the shell where she did.

Okay? Okay. I think that just about covers everything. So let's get back (which is really moving on, because it happened later) to Eddie and his mother, on crutches, walking up the drive to Awful End, that cold winter's afternoon.

'You want me to go to America?' said Eddie, in amazement.

5

No, hang on. Wait a minute. I thought I'd just about covered everything in the how-she-came-to-drop-the-mortar-shell incident, but there are two glaring omissions (things left out). Firstly; who put the shell in the sewing box; and, secondly, what it was that Mrs Dickens tripped over, causing her to throw the shell in the first place. Both can be easily explained.

The shell had been a present to Mad Uncle Jack from a local shopkeeper who didn't like him. He secretly rather hoped that MUJ would keep it over the fireplace and the heat would cause it to explode, giving Mad Uncle Jack a headache and an expensive repair bill, at the very least. That would teach him not to squish fruit and vegetables when he had no intention of buying them! Mad Uncle Jack had, indeed, put this fine, gleaming, brass mortar shell on display on one of the many mantelpieces in Awful End, but it had caught the eye of his loving wife, Even Madder Aunt Maud.

Even Madder Aunt Maud was a woman who acted on impulse. The day she first set eyes on a stuffed stoat, whom she later called Malcolm, she fell in love with him and he became her (almost) constant companion. The day she saw the snout of a hollow cow sticking over a hedgerow, her heart went all a flutter once again, and she knew there and then that she would call the cow Marjorie and live inside her.

When she saw the gleaming shell case, she wanted it. I've no idea what for. She never said and, though I give a very good impression of one once in a while, when I write 'he thought' or 'she wondered', I'm not a state-registered mind reader. All I know is she wanted it, picked it up and was horrified to see that her hands left fingermarks and palm prints on the nice brass, which might tarnish the lovely gleam which had attracted her to it in the first place. She needed something to carry it in. She went into the nearest room and there, on a stool by the window, sat Mrs Dickens's sewing box. Not only was it just the right size, it also had a *handy carrying handle*.

Even Madder Aunt Maud tipped the contents out of the box, and swept them out of the way with her feet, under an old upright piano, putting the shell in the box. She was just about to carry it out to Marjorie, when she remembered that she'd left Malcolm the stuffed stoat on the mantelpiece. It was as she dashed out to retrieve him that Eddie's mum walked in and found the shell in the sewing box. It was just a case of bad luck and bad timing. If she hadn't wanted to sew up that gap in the curtain, or had come in a moment sooner and been able to ask Aunt Maud what she was up to, or come in *later*, allowing time for Even Madder Aunt Maud to have retrieved Malcolm and taken the sewing box, Mrs Dickens wouldn't be in the poor state she was in now.

Which only leaves the matter of what she tripped over, mortar shell in hand: a now-empty pot which had once contained green paint. And I don't think *that* requires further explanation!

Immediately after the explosion, Mad Uncle Jack dashed down the ladder from his tree house, three rungs at a time. Eddie, who was helping Dawkins polish the family silver, dashed out of the kitchen door and around the side of the house. Mr Dickens fell out of a laburnum tree he'd been painting, and Gibbering Jane (their retired/failed chambermaid) stayed under the stairs. Even Madder Aunt Maud was the last to appear, clutching Malcolm under her arm, and still frowning a puzzled frown at the sudden disappearance of the sewing box and shell.

Mad Uncle Jack, Eddie and Dawkins all ran to assist Mrs Dickens, whilst Even Madder Aunt Maud ambled over to Mr Dickens, who was lying on his back, moaning. She held Malcolm by the tail and prodded Eddie's father with the stuffed stoat's nose. 'What's all the fuss about, ay?' she demanded.

Meanwhile, Eddie's mum just groaned a lot and looked a bit crumpled. Back then, it wasn't simply a matter of picking up a phone and calling an ambulance. Dawkins was sent into town, on horseback, to find the doctor and it was a good hour before both men came galloping back. By then, Even Madder Aunt Maud had made the gruesome discovery of the ex-ex-soldier. Death is never nice, even in books. She told Mad Uncle Jack, who was able to identify which of his men it was – he still thought of them that way, and they did often do odd-jobs around the house – by a medal, still hot and slightly melted – in a flowerbed. On it were the words:

BEST OF BREED

9

'It was Gorey,' he said quietly. 'Poor chap.'

Doctor Humple took one look at Eddie's mother and assured her that she'd be fine in next to no time. He gave her the neck brace straight from his bag and arranged for crutches to be delivered, and had her up and walking about in a matter of days. Eddie's father was less lucky. The fall from the tree had hurt his back and, even as our story starts that following winter, he spent most of the time lying on his back, unable to sit up, let alone walk.

'I don't think the author likes me,' he once muttered. 'I always seem to get injured in these books.' Of course, none of the other characters had any idea what he was talking about.

It was soon after the accident that Eddie's father had a brilliant idea. He'd remembered reading somewhere about a famous artist called Michel Angelo, whom he assumed would have been called 'Mike Angel' if he'd been an Englishman – in fact 'Michelangelo' was just the artist's first name, his surname was Buonarroti – who'd painted the ceiling of a place called the Sistine Chapel. Mr Buonarroti had covered it with pictures of clouds and angels, and Adam and Eve and suchlike . . . but he'd done it all from wooden scaffolding, built to the height of just below the ceiling, and had painted the whole thing whilst lying on his back!

So, rather than lying around feeling sorry for himself, Mr Dickens had the remaining ex-soldiers build him a wooden scaffolding rig on wheels, and he started to paint the ceiling of the great hall in Awful End. His food was brought up and his chamber pot taken down. Occasionally, Gibbering Jane would clamber up and give him a sponge bath or one of the family would join him for a while to keep him company, or mix him new coloured paints. When he'd finished painting one patch of roof, they'd simply wheel the whole wooden scaffolding rig forward about a foot, and on he'd go.

There's a phrase about making triumph out of adversity, which has nothing to do with the saying about making a silk purse out of a pig's ear (natural causes or no natural causes). It means making something good out of something bad . . . and that's exactly what Mr Dickens would have done – produced a work of art when his bad back prevented him from doing just about anything else – were it not for the fact that he couldn't paint to save his life. Painting leaves on trees a brighter colour was where Eddie's dad's talent ended. If he actually tried to paint something to look like a leaf, it looked as much like an angel as his angels did, which was *not much*.

The ceiling in the great hall looked dreadful.

No, worse than that. If an unsuspecting visitor entered Awful End through the main entrance and saw the ceiling without warning, he might think that either some strange and horrifying multicoloured fungus had spread across it, or he'd eaten some mushrooms that hadn't agreed with him and was having weird and crazy hallucinations. Mr Dickens's ceiling was horrible. Today, it's painted over with several layers of very thick white paint. How very sensible.

. . . Which reminds me of the thick white snow on the ground as Eddie and his mother walked up the drive to Awful End and she raised the subject of America.

'America?' said Eddie in amazement. 'You want me to go to America?'

His mother managed a little nod, despite her huge whalebone-and-linen surgical collar. 'Well, I can't go like this, and your father can't even tie his own shoelaces the state he's still in, so, yes, I'm asking you to go to America for us. Your great-uncle will explain everything.'

Wow! This sounded the sort of adventure Eddie really could enjoy.

Episode 2

A Painful Surprise

In which Mad Uncle Jack gets it in the end and Even Madder Aunt Maud has an attack of guilt

Eddie found Mad Uncle Jack in his study, crouching under his large oak desk in the space meant for his knees.

'It's very roomy in here!' he announced on seeing his grand-nephew. 'Very roomy indeed . . . so roomy, in fact, I think I shall make a room of it.'

Before Eddie knew what was happening, Mad Uncle Jack had leapt to his feet and was brandishing a small ceremonial sword. Eddie remembered Mad Uncle Jack telling him that he'd been given it by some surrendering foreign general, long before Eddie had been born.

'I shall cut a hole for a window in the back, fit a door to the front and – hey presto – a new room just like that!'

Eddie knew better than to ask Mad Uncle Jack where he proposed to fit his knees the next time he tried to sit down at the desk.

'How nice,' said Eddie, instead.

'This is just what I need to cheer me up!' his great-uncle pronounced.

'Why do you need cheering up?' asked Eddie. MUJ seemed perfectly cheerful to him.

'With poor Gorey dead, your mother on crutches and your father up that wooden contraption of his, need you ask, dear boy?' he said, which was a surprisingly sensible thing for him to say.

Eddie seized the moment of sanity and said what he'd come in for. 'Mother says you want me to go to America,' but Mad Uncle Jack was no longer listening.

He was crawling back under the desk – head first this time – and starting to stab the wooden board at the back with the ceremonial sword. He made a high-pitched whine with every thrust: '*Aieeeeeeeeeeeeeeeeeeeeeeeeeeeee!!!*'

At that very moment – I added the word 'very'

15

because I suspect I often use the phrase 'at that moment' in Eddie Dickens books, so I wanted to disguise it a little – Even Madder Aunt Maud entered the room by opening a window and stepping in, shaking the snow from the elephant's-foot-umbrella-stand she was wearing as a boot on each foot.

She took one look at her husband's posterior protruding – that's 'bottom sticking out' to you and me – from beneath the desk and dashed (as fast as her elephant's-foot umbrella-stands would allow her) across the study to the fireplace. Grabbing a brass toasting fork from a selection of fireside utensils, she thrust it into MUJ's buttock. It was his left, I believe, though there were to be conflicting accounts later.

'BURGLAR!' she cried, so loudly that it almost drowned out the roar of pain and surprise coming from beneath the desk, which is really saying something!

Technically, of course, she was inaccurate. 'Burglars' do their burgling at night. In the daytime, such a person should have been called a 'housebreaker'. Then again, she was being even more inaccurate than that, wasn't she? (That was what we call a rhetorical question. I don't expect you to answer me. You're probably too far away for me to hear, anyway.) Mad Uncle Jack was neither burglar nor housebreaker. He was her husband! It was at times like these that Eddie wondered if he wouldn't be better off living in a nice quiet orphanage somewhere.

Mad Uncle Jack emerged from under the desk red-faced and enraged, his hat crumpled like a concertina (which may not be a very original simile, but is a jolly good one, along with 'as black as a bruised banana').

'WHAT IS GOING ON?' he demanded, pulling the prongs – or 'tines' if you want to be ever so accurate – of the toasting fork from his bottom.

To Eddie's utter amazement, Even Madder Aunt Maud actually looked apologetic. He'd expected her to be unrepentant, blaming her husband for being under the desk in the first place, or 'masquerading as a burglar' or something. But no. She looked positively sheepish at having pronged – or tined – poor Mad Uncle Jack.

'My sweet!' she cried, in anguish, tossing

17

Malcolm aside and throwing her arms around her injured man.

Fortunately for Eddie, he managed to catch the stuffed stoat as he came flying through the air like some thick French breadstick used as a throwing club. Eddie knew from experience that being hit by a flying Malcolm was enough to knock a fleeing convict to the ground.

Jack and Maud's hug had somehow taken on the appearance of a grapple. Losing her footing in her elephant's-foot umbrella-stand boots, Even Madder Aunt Maud was trying to use her husband to steady herself at the same time he was using her to steady *himself* as he tried to turn to inspect the damage done to his behind. The result? A terrible crash and an entanglement of Great-uncle and Great-aunt on the bearskin rug in front of the spluttering study fire. I'd love to say that the fire was 'roaring' but Mad Uncle Jack spent most of the time living in a treehouse in the garden so the fire was rarely lit. When it was, families of hibernating mice or hedgehogs had to be carefully moved some place else first, and the wood was often damp and spitting.

(If you know about real fires, you'll know about spitting logs. If you don't, you'll just have to take my word for it: a damp or sappy log can spit like an angry camel but, unlike camels, they don't – according to folklore – know the 100th name of Allah, so don't have that all-knowing smug expression that camels do, which you'd have too if you knew such an important and sacred name. In fact, most logs' expressions – big or small – are quite wooden.)

And don't think I have forgotten about the poor old bear who ended up as a bearskin rug on the floor. Back in Eddie's day, animal-skin rugs were everywhere: lions, tigers, bears of all shapes and sizes. It was unusual to stand on a rug that hadn't once been running around quite happily in the sunshine. I don't know this particular bear's history but I'm sorry to say that he probably ended more with a bang than with all his family around his bed (in the bear cave) as he ended his days saying, 'I've had a good life . . .'

Which brings us back to Mad Uncle Jack lying on top of his ruggy (as opposed to rugged) remains.

'Are you all right?' asked Eddie, helping his great-aunt to her feet.

'What have I done? What have I done?' she groaned.

They both looked down at Mad Uncle Jack who lay there like a helpless upturned beetle.

'I'm sure he'll be fine,' said Eddie, trying to sound reassuring. He took MUJ by the arm and tried to help him to his feet.

'Leave me,' he whispered hoarsely into the boy's ear. 'You must get word to Fort Guana.'

'Fort Guana?' asked a puzzled Eddie.

'Tell them that we will hold the ridge until re-enforcements arrive . . .' He paused and took a gulp of air. 'The Bumbaloonies shall not break through our ranks!' He turned his face away and came eye-to-glass-eye with the head of the bearskin rug.

'I see that Corporal Muggins didn't make it,' he sighed, stroking the head. 'A fine soldier. Made an excellent omelette.' He turned back to Eddie, tears in his eyes. 'It's all down to you now, my boy . . . Take my horse . . .' and, with that, he fainted.

Snatching Malcolm from the occasional table where Eddie had placed him, Even Madder Aunt Maud let out a truly dreadful cry of despair and fled the study – this time through the doorway rather than the window.

Eddie looked at the unconscious form of Mad Uncle Jack. He didn't think that he'd be finding out much more about his trip to America that day!

Episode 3

A Cure for Ills?

*In which Doctor Humple pays yet another visit to
Awful End and Eddie goes in search of shiny things*

As it turned out, Doctor Humple was more
concerned about Mad Aunt Maud's state of
health than Mad Uncle Jack's. After a good night's
rest and a few of Dr Humple's large blue pills,
Eddie's great-uncle seemed to be back to his same
old self, apart from a sore bottom, backache and
a slight limp. The doctor had tucked him up in his
tree house (which was made entirely from
creosoted dried fish) and, by the next morning,
he'd been down the ladder and building snow

sculptures like he did most winter mornings, weather permitting.

Even Madder Aunt Maud, in her hollow cow in the rose garden, meanwhile, was far from her normal self. She clutched Malcolm to her, rocking backwards and forwards, muttering, 'What have I done? What have I done?' and no amount of coaxing could get her to relax and unwind.

Once Eddie's mother had taken to regularly eating raw onions and, after the habit had passed, Even Madder Aunt Maud had threaded the remaining vegetables singly – like conkers – and hung them at different heights from Marjorie's 'ceiling'. There was nothing she liked more than passing the dark evenings by hitting the suspended onions with Malcolm's nose, singing as she went; as though each onion somehow represented a particular musical note.

Eddie tried hitting them and singing now – there was no way that he could prise Malcolm from her grasp, so he'd used a wooden spoon. No reaction. Even Madder Aunt Maud simply continued to snivel. Even Dr Humple's mixture of big blue, small pink and medium-sized yellow pills had no effect. Even Madder Aunt Maud was awash with guilt at stabbing and then knocking out her beloved Jack.

They brought Mad Uncle Jack to see her, to

show her that he was, in his own words, 'as right as rain'(apart from the sore bottom, backache and slight limp, in the *other* leg now) but this made no difference. She was still terribly upset. MUJ soon grew tired of trying to 'make her snap out of it' – his words again – so he stomped off back through the snow to his treehouse, in a huff.

Dr Humple put his arm on Eddie's shoulder. 'I really am at a loss as to how to help your poor great-aunt, at present,' he said. 'Fortunately for us, Time is the great healer.'

Although Eddie was hearing the words come from the doctor's mouth, rather than seeing them on the printed page as you are, he knew that Dr Humple had just said 'Time' with a capital 'T', in the same way that people sometimes say 'Nature' with a capital 'N', when they mean Nature in an all-important way . . .

. . . From past experience, Eddie knew that Mad Aunt Maud's mood could certainly change in the time it took to blink an eye or scratch an eyebrow, but a mood change didn't necessarily make things better. Suddenly, an idea popped into his head.

'Shiny things!' he said.

The doctor stopped what he was doing – which was coiling up his stethoscope and putting it in his top hat (that's where doctors used to keep their

stethoscopes. Honestly, dear reader, I promise) –
and stared at Eddie. 'What do you mean by shiny
things, my boy?' he asked.

'Well, you remember when you came in the
summer and gave Mother the neck brace and
crutches and Father the back-strengthening corset?'

'How could I forget?' said Dr Humple. 'They're
both still using them . . . and that was the day poor
Gorey died, beneath the spreading rhubarb
leaves.'

'Exactly!' Eddie continued. 'The whole thing
came about because Even Madder Aunt Maud –'
He paused and looked down at his great-aunt,
whom they'd managed to tuck up in bed, but
seemed oblivious to (unaware of) what was going
on around her. 'The whole dreadful accident
happened because Mad Aunt Maud liked the look
of a shiny artillery shell.'

'The idea is to make the poor lady feel less guilty
about herself, young Edmund, not MORE!' the
doctor reminded him.

'No, you don't understand,' said Eddie
hurriedly. 'I was simply about to suggest that we
try to distract her with some new shiny object she
might like.'

'Aha!' said Dr Humple, his hat back on his
head, the stethoscope safely tucked inside (his hat,
not his head). 'That is, indeed, clever thinking!'

25

'Shall I go up to the house and see if I can find something really shiny?' Eddie suggested.

'An excellent idea!' said the doctor. 'In the meantime I shall check her pulse.'

Eddie slipped out of Marjorie's bottom – she was the carnival float cow they were in, remember – and crunched his way through the snow towards the back of Awful End.

He was surprised to see Gibbering Jane taking down some washing from the line near the kitchen door. As a failed chambermaid, Jane usually spent her time under the stairs, sitting in the dark, knitting her life away. When Eddie's previous home had burnt down, all she'd managed to save of her years of knitting was the charred corner of an egg cosy which she, thereafter, wore on a piece of string around her neck. She'd moved to Awful End with Eddie's parents and gentleman's gentleman Dawkins . . . directly under the stairs there, so it was unusual to see her doing anything as ordinary as bring in the washing. Not that it was straightforward. The temperature had dropped considerably overnight, and the clothes were as stiff as boards. Put a shirt above a pair of trousers, and it would look as though a very flat person was inside them.

Gibbering Jane gibbered as she tried to bend the clothes to fit inside the wicker washing basket.

She was fighting a losing battle. When she saw Eddie, she dropped the basket – a rigid sock sticking in the snow like a knitted boomerang – and ran (you guessed it) still gibbering into the house. By the time Eddie had entered the warm glow of the kitchen, he could hear the door under the stairs slamming shut.

Eddie's mum, Mrs Dickens, was sitting at the kitchen table, cutting the crusts off a pile of triangular sandwiches with a pair of carpet scissors.

'Hello, Jonathan.' She beamed when she saw her son. (Don't ask.)

'Hello, Mother,' said Eddie.

'I'm making these for your father's breakfast,' she said.

If you're trying to work out what time of day it was, don't let the whole breakfast business put you off. We're in the DICKENS household, remember. Breakfast could be served at any time during a twenty-four-hour period (if at all) depending upon who was doing the serving.

'How is Father?' asked Eddie, who hadn't climbed up the scaffolding in the hall for the past few days.

'Having great difficulty drawing the serpent in the Garden of Eden,' said Mrs Dickens. 'Apparently, it keeps coming out looking like a liver sausage.'

'Oh,' said Eddie, who secretly thought that his father's paintings of both Adam and Eve looked rather like liver sausages, too.

'Would you like something to eat?' asked his mother. 'There are plenty of crusts.' She trimmed another sandwich, adding the crusts to an already impressive pile.

'No, thank you,' said Eddie. 'I'm actually looking for something shiny . . . something which might distract poor Even Madder Aunt Maud from feeling so guilty about stabbing and knocking out Mad Uncle Jack.'

'Poor Jack,' said Mrs Dickens, placing the carpet scissors on the table and dabbing her eyes with the corner of a lacy hanky she kept up her sleeve. 'We shall all miss him so.'

'Miss him? But he's alive and well, Mother!' Eddie protested. 'He was with us inside Marjorie just now, trying to comfort Even Madder Aunt Maud.'

'Then whose funeral did I attend the other day?' asked Mrs Dickens, a confused look passing across her handsome features.

Funeral? There hadn't been any funerals lately. The last time Eddie could remember seeing a coffin was when he'd ended up in one, in the book called *Dreadful Acts* (not that he'd realised that he was in a book called *Dreadful Acts*, or called anything else, for that matter). Then he remembered the hen.

Dawkins kept hens for their eggs, one of which (hen not egg) Mad Aunt Maud was particularly fond of. Sadly she had died of old age a few days previously. Maud had insisted that Ethel, the chicken, be buried, and all members of the (human) family had been required to attend the brief service.

'You're not thinking of the chicken's funeral are you, Mother?' Eddie asked.

'Why, of course! How silly of me,' said Mrs Dickens, trimming the final sandwich and arranging the pile neatly on the plate. 'An easy mistake. They're both so plump and feathery.'

Eddie could see how Mad Uncle Jack's whiskeriness might be compared to feathers, but plump? He was about as thin as a person could be and still be classified as a person. Any thinner and he might be a stick man . . . but Eddie knew better than to say anything. He decided to resume his quest for something shiny.

*

Eddie finally found just what he was looking for in one of the upstairs rooms that nobody used any more. It had once contained furniture covered in white sheets, to stop it getting dusty. That had been done back in the days when Mad Uncle Jack and Even Madder Aunt Maud had an army of servants. Now they were all gone and – before Eddie and his parents had moved in with Dawkins and Gibbering Jane – all they'd been left with was the very small army of retired army misfits (of whom 'Best of Breed' Private Gorey had been one). Over the years, MUJ and EMAM – oooh, that's the first time I've used EMAM, and I like it! – had used the furniture under the white sheets as firewood, and used the white sheets as sheets, or to play 'ghosts'.

(By the way, I should explain that there was a fashion for calling people by their initials . . . and not necessarily their own. Don't ask me why, but the Victorian prime minister William Gladstone, for example, was often referred to as GOM, meaning 'Grand Old Man'; so my MUJs and EMAMs fit quite neatly into the period, thank you.)

When Eddie entered the room, it was bare; bare floor, bare walls, bare ceiling . . . well, not quite a bare ceiling for, although there were no carpets or rugs on the floor and no paintings or fixtures on the walls, from the middle of the ceiling hung a huge chandelier, glinting in the weak winter sunlight that had managed to make it through the slats of the closed shutters across the windows.

Most of the chandelier was covered in years of dust, and was loosely wrapped in what looked like a giant hairnet, but it still managed to wink in places at Eddie, as if to share the secret that brilliant cut-glass crystal lay beneath. From the bottom of the chandelier, nestling in the net, hung a glass bauble the size of an orange. Eddie felt sure that if he could reach this bauble, unhook it and polish it, it would be just the kind of shiny object to fascinate his great-aunt. The problem was the first part: reaching it. He looked around for something to stand on. Zilch. Zero. Then he remembered the library steps his mother kept in the bathroom for diving practice and he hurried off to find them.

By the time that Eddie was striding back down towards Marjorie, through the snow, the crystal-cut bauble in his gloved hand was sparkling and glinting like the world's biggest diamond. Eddie wasn't wearing the gloves to keep out the cold, but to keep from smudging the bauble. He didn't want a few fingerprints to spoil what he hoped would be the effect this shiny thing would have on Even Madder Aunt Maud.

Episode 4

A Brief Family History

*In which Eddie learns more about
his family and the reasons for going to America*

Eddie's mind wasn't entirely on curing Mad Aunt Maud as he stamped the snow off his shoes and clambered inside Marjorie. He was still thinking about the trip to America, whatever that was about. If only his mother or Mad Uncle Jack had had a chance to explain things to him before Mad Uncle Jack and Even Madder Aunt Maud had joined the list of casualties.

Dr Humple was giving the boy's great-aunt another large blue pill, with a sip of water from a glass when Eddie entered.

'What are in those pills, Doctor?' Eddie asked.

'The large blue ones?'

Eddie nodded.

'Mainly blue dye. It's very expensive, which is why my bills are so high . . . What's that amazing jewel you have there?' Dr Humple was eyeing the crystal-cut bauble the size of an orange, nestling in Eddie's gloved hands.

'A shiny thing!' said Eddie, passing it to the doctor.

Dr Humple held it up in front of Even Madder Aunt Maud, just out of her reach. She sat bolt upright in bed and tried to snatch it. The doctor jerked his hand away. 'I think it's working, Eddie!' said the doctor, obviously impressed.

'Ah, my precious!' said Even Madder Aunt Maud, which would have been a quote from a character called Golom in a book called *The Hobbit*, except that *The Hobbit* hadn't been written yet, which made Even Madder Aunt Maud way, way, way ahead of her time.

Even Madder Aunt Maud made another swipe for the bauble and Dr Humple almost dropped it. He fumblingly saved it from falling to the floor and tossed it over to Eddie who caught it with ease. His great-aunt was out of the bed now, clutching Malcolm by the tail, but she only had eyes for one item: the shiny thing.

She launched herself at Eddie who stood by the opening in Marjorie's bottom, and threw the crystal-cut bauble out into the garden, aiming for the deepest snowdrift so as not to damage it.

Even Madder Aunt Maud bounded after it like a dog after a ball thrown by its master. And it should remind anyone who's read *Dreadful Acts* of a certain escaped convict who seemed to think he was a hound.

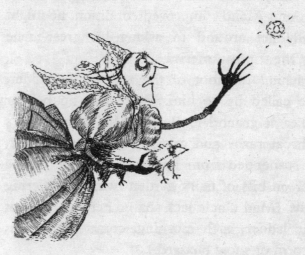

'Well, Master Edmund,' said the doctor, 'she's up and about again, but now what?'

'You're the doctor,' said Eddie. 'Shouldn't you decide?'

Dr Humple and Eddie watched Even Madder Aunt Maud dig the bauble out of the snowdrift and hold it triumphantly to the sky.

'Well,' said the doctor hesitantly, 'she seems fine to me. Fully cured.'

'Certainly back to her old self,' Eddie agreed.

Dr Humple stepped out of the hollow cow. 'Why don't you go and tell your great-uncle the excellent news?' he suggested. 'And please inform him that I shall be sending him my bill in due course.'

Eddie hurried off through the snow to Mad Uncle Jack's treehouse. Once he'd told him about Mad Aunt Maud's improved condition, he might actually get around to asking his great-uncle about the trip to America.

Reaching the foot of the tree house ladder, Eddie called up to him. There was no bell or knocker at ground level, just Mad Uncle Jack's cut-throat razor and a piece of broken mirror, each suspended from hooks in the side of the ladder on bits of hairy garden twine of differing lengths. (Mad Uncle Jack shaved here, at the foot of the ladder, each morning, come rain, shine, hailstorm or snow blizzard.)

'Uncle Jack!' Eddie called. 'Uncle Jack?'

The beakiest of beaky noses appeared through an unglazed window up above. An unglazed window is a window without any glass in it, which means that it's really just another phrase for a hole. The word 'window' actually comes from the Old Norse word *vindauga* which means 'wind eye' – useful for keeping an eye on the wind – and Old Norse windows certainly didn't have glass in them either.

'Who is it?' Mad Uncle Jack called down.

36

'Eddie!'

'What's the password?' Mad Uncle Jack shouted.

Eddie sighed. He'd never needed a password to be allowed up into the tree house before, so why now? 'I didn't know there was one!' he groaned.

'Correct!' cried Mad Uncle Jack triumphantly. 'Come on up, my boy! Come on up!'

A somewhat relieved Eddie shinned up the ladder. (People often shin up ladders in books. Have you noticed that? They sometimes shin up drainpipes, too . . . but you very rarely get people shinning up stairs.)

Mad Uncle Jack was delighted to see Eddie. 'Come in and sit yourself down,' he said. 'You're probably here to ask me about the American trip, aren't you?'

Mad Uncle Jack was sitting on one of the elephant's-foot umbrella-stands that Even Madder Aunt Maud had been using as a boot. 'Yes,' said Eddie. He sat himself down on a small upturned wooden crate marked 'MANGOES'. Behind his great-uncle was a bed and between them a rather wobbly table, and that was about all there was room for in the tree house. 'And also to tell you that Even Madder Aunt Maud is back to her old self again.'

'Oh dear,' said Mad Uncle Jack. 'I'm very sorry to hear that.' Eddie didn't know what to say, so he

37

wisely said nothing. 'Well, before I explain what I
– what *we* – need you to do in America, I think I
should give you a little Dickens family history,'
said his great-uncle, at last.

'Fine.' Eddie nodded, hoping beyond hope that
Mad Uncle Jack wouldn't get too side-tracked.

'Your Great-uncle George is probably the most
famous of the recent Dickenses,' MUJ began,
tilting back on the elephant's foot. 'He burnt
down the Houses of Parliament in 1834, which is
why we have the nice new gothicy one with Big
Ben and all . . .'

'You mean your brother George was a kind of
Guy Fawkes?' gasped Eddie.

'What, the gunpowder, treason and plot chap? I
think the difference is that Guy Fawkes *planned* to
burn down the Houses of Parliament and *didn't*,
and Brother George *didn't* plan to burn down the
Houses of Parliament . . .'

'But *did*!' said Eddie, in amazement. 'So it was
an accident! Did he get into trouble?'

'Of course not,' said Mad Uncle Jack.

'Why not?' asked Eddie. He imagined that
burning down the Houses of Parliament, by
mistake or not, would be a getting-into-serious-
trouble offence.

'Because he never told anybody in authority,'
said MUJ. 'That's why.'

'So he's only famous in the family for having done it? Not the history books?'

'Exactly,' said his great-uncle. 'But that's no less an achievement. If it hadn't been for my brother, we wouldn't have that fabulous new building with all the twiddly bits.'

'How did he – er – accidentally set fire to the old Parliament building?' Eddie asked. 'A smouldering cigar butt, a casually discarded match?'

'Over-zealous stoking,' said Mad Uncle Jack. 'It could have happened to anybody. It was the sixteenth of October – George's birthday – and, as a treat, a friend of his sneaked him into the Parliament's boiler room to let him help stoke the furnaces.

'Even as a boy, George was mad keen on fire, you know. Nothing he loved more than a smouldering carpet or a blazing curtain. Set fire to local tradespeople on numerous occasions, when we were lads, but always in the spirit of fun! They stopped calling at the house. They've always lacked humour, the lower classes.'

'And this friend of his let him stoke the furnaces underneath Parliament?!' said Eddie, in disbelief.

'As I said, it was his birthday . . . Anyhow, Brother George over-fed the furnaces. He filled them up with much too much stuff . . . far too many tally sticks.'

'Tally whats?'

'No, tally sticks. Right up until the twenties, the government used wooden sticks, rather than paper or dried fish, to work out tax. By 1834, the practice was as dead as Private Gorey and they were using them as firewood –'

'And Great Uncle George stuffed too many into the furnaces?' asked Eddie, trying to get a clear picture of events.

Mad Uncle Jack tried to suppress a giggle. 'I'm afraid so. George says it was a beautiful sight, the orange flames and smoke blowing out across the River Thames.'

'Didn't he feel guilty?' said Eddie.

Mad Uncle Jack nodded. 'Not for long though.

He was killed soon after.'

'Set fire to himself?'

'No, as a result of an accident arising from his conviction that he was a fish,' Eddie's great-uncle explained. 'He took to living in a large tank in a rented space near the Manufacturers Museum and – refusing to come up for air one Thursday – he died.' (Today the museum is called the V & A.)

Eddie looked around the inside of the tree house made of dried fish, and thought of the rockpool dug into the floor of the study. What was it about the Dickens family and fish? Great Uncle George had died thinking he was one, and Mad [Great] Uncle Jack even tried to *pay* for everything with dried fish! He wondered whether Grandpa Percy had ever had any fishy habits, too.

For those of you who might doubt Mad Uncle Jack's claims – and why not, he's not been the most reliable of people throughout the trilogy, has he? – I should say that the Houses of Parliament in London were indeed destroyed by fire in 1834 *and* as a result of overloading the furnaces with tally sticks, though whether his brother really had a part in it I can't say. From his childhood behaviour, it seems just the sort of thing he would have done, though.

Fortunately, London had formed its first single fire service the year before the fire. Prior to that, if your house caught alight it would only have been put out by the firemen (they were all men) working for the particular insurance company your house was insured with. Otherwise, they'd just stand there on the other side of the road and watch.

A couple of important bits of the old buildings were saved: the Great Hall (which was great) and the Jewel Tower (which was good news, too). This was partly thanks to the London Fire Engine Establishment (the fire brigade) and partly thanks to a chap called Lord Melbourne who happened to be Prime Minister at the time, so was good at being bossy, and told the firemen what to do. These old bits were incorporated into the new building which is still there today (or, at the very least, at the time I'm writing this).

'I met Chance, once, you know,' said Mad Uncle Jack, picking up the dried swordfish he used as a letter opener from the rickety table, and sticking the tip of its nose into his ear, giving it a quick joggle. 'An itch,' he explained on seeing Eddie's startled expression.

'Who was Chance?' asked Eddie.

'A dog belonging to the Watling Street Fire Station,' said Mad Uncle Jack. 'Born for search and rescue work, he was. No one had to train him. He would dash up the escape ladder into a burning building and start hunting for survivors.

If he found someone, he'd sniff out his master and bark to tell him that someone was in trouble. Saved lots of lives, he did. Quite the hero.'

Eddie looked doubtful but, amazingly, his great-uncle was telling the truth. Chance was a bit of a celebrity in his day and wore a special collar with a message on it which read: '*Stop me not but onward let me jog, for I am the London firemen's dog.*'

Chance's life is just the sort of thing which will get made into one of those children's feel-good costume-drama programmes they put on television around Christmas time, mark my words. And when it does, you can say, 'I know where they pinched the idea from; that nice Mr Ardagh and his brilliant book *Terrible Times*,' and you can write to the TV company and demand that I get a special payment for coming up with it.

What Mad Uncle Jack didn't mention (and probably didn't know) and the television programme might, possibly, leave out is that – after his death – Chance was stuffed and shown off at fairgrounds . . . which wasn't the most dignified end for such a heroic hound.

'Er . . . what does your dead brother George have to do with my going to America, Mad Uncle Jack?' Eddie asked, trying to steer the topic of conversation back on course.

The empty mango crate wasn't the most comfortable seat in the world and, anyhow, it was getting cold in the tree house.

'My father had three sons,' Mad Uncle Jack explained. 'There was my elder brother George. There was me – if there hadn't been, he wouldn't have been my father, now, would he? – and there was my younger brother Percy, who was your grandfather.'

'Father has a picture of him in his room,' Eddie recalled. His parents' room at Awful End wasn't the one they'd first occupied when they moved into the house. That had been damaged in a gas explosion. Though the damage had been repaired, it had been repaired by Mad Uncle Jack's faithful ragbag of ex-soldiers . . . which brings the word 'repair' into question, if not disrepute. So Mr and Mrs Dickens had moved into another, smaller room and it was there, by their wash-stand, that the small portrait of Grandpa Percy hung.

He was from the very heavily bearded era of Queen Victoria's reign. Percy Dickens was more beard than just about anything else. You could just make out the eyes and there was a hint of a nose in there somewhere, but it would be a complete waste of time searching for a mouth, though it must have been *somewhere* under all that facial hair. Despite being all beard – he needn't have worn a collar and tie, for example, because the bushiness of the beard hid all of his neck and most of his torso down to his tummy button – he still managed to look stern in the portrait, which is quite an achievement when you consider there was little room for any features. Whenever Eddie looked at the picture, he imagined his grandfather was being disapproving or saying 'no!' to something; anything; *everything*.

'What was he like, Uncle Jack?' asked Eddie.

MUJ shook his head, sadly. 'Percy was a very strange boy,' he said. 'He showed no interest in fish, the army, or any of the games George and I played as children. He always had his nose stuck in a book. I don't mean that he did a great deal of reading. I simply mean that he had his nose stuck in a book . . . the same book, and stuck between the same two pages for about thirty-two years. He even slept that way, which made him prone to snoring and, if he ever got a cold, you can imagine how soggy that book became after all that sneezing and constant nose-dripping.'

'But why did he do that?' asked Eddie, wondering if anyone in the world had normal relatives or whether all families were secretly barmy.

'I've absolutely no idea, m'boy,' said Mad Uncle Jack. 'I never thought to ask him.'

Eddie sighed. Why did grown-ups never ask the sort of questions any sensible ordinary kid would? 'Can you remember what the book was?' he asked.

Eddie's great-uncle tilted precariously on the elephant's foot, the back of his head brushing against the creosoted fish wall. 'Of course I can!' he said indignantly, then fell silent. (Why people *fall* silent rather than *go* silent is one of those

46

mysteries, like why wire coat-hangers multiply if left alone long enough in a wardrobe: you start off with six and, by the following month, you end up with a tangle of about four hundred and twenty-eight.)

Eddie waited for Mad Uncle Jack to tell him the book's title. Nothing. 'Er, what was it?' he asked, when he could bear it no longer.

'Oh, *Old Roxbee's Compendium of All Knowledge: Volume Three*,' said Mad Uncle Jack. 'Of course, I've no idea what it was about because I could never get it off Percy. He was too busy sticking his nose in it.'

Eddie reflected on that generation of Dickenses. Three brothers: George, the arsonist, Jack, the general all-round nutter, and Percy the man with the book on his face . . .

What had the neighbours thought? How had they coped in polite society? The truth be told, a lot of the upper classes in those days were a bit bonkers but, *because* they were upper class, they were called 'eccentric' and everyone thought, 'Oh, that's all right, then.'

After another period of silence, Eddie asked: 'What does your telling me about your brothers George and Percy have to do with your wanting me to travel to America?'

'Good question!' said Uncle Jack, picking up the stuffed swordfish for a second time, this time employing it as a back-scratcher. (I don't mean 'employing' it as in putting it on the payroll and giving it a regular wage – what would be the point of paying a dead fish? – but employing as in using . . . which means that if I'd simply employed the word used, or should that be used the word used, I wouldn't be in this mess now.) 'In fact, an excellent question!' he continued. 'You see our father, Dr Malcontent Dickens, had a number of interests in America, the most important of which was the ownership of a newspaper which was not afraid of telling the news as it really was. It was – and still is – called the *Terrible Times* and has an extremely high readership, I am informed, on the Eastern Seaboard.'

Eddie had no idea what the Eastern Seaboard

was, so he asked his great-uncle, who had no idea either.

'Sounds rather like a sideboard to me, only larger,' he said. 'Everything in America is larger. I'm told the mice are the size of rats and the rats are the size of dogs.'

'What about the dogs?' Eddie asked, wondering how big they might be (so as not to be confused with the rats).

'What about them?' asked Mad Uncle Jack.

'Oh, nothing,' said Eddie. 'You were telling me about the *Terrible Times*.'

'Was I? I mean, I was. It was originally my father's newspaper, then, when he was killed by the human cannon ball, it was passed on to us three boys. George never married so, when he died, his share was divided in two and passed on to me and young Percy, so we both owned half the paper. Then, when your Grandpa Percy died, his share went to your father.'

'So you and Father own a daily newspaper in America called the *Terrible Times*?' he said, making a mental note to ask him about the human cannon ball another time, because he didn't want to risk getting off the main subject now.

'Exactly,' nodded Mad Uncle Jack, his beak-like nose casting an interestingly shaped shadow on the tree house wall.

'And you don't just mean a copy of an old newspaper, you mean a company which produces a newspaper every day –'

'Except Sundays,' his great-uncle interjected (which, in this case, is the same as interrupting).

'– except Sundays – which is read by a large number of people on the Eastern Seaboard –'

'Whatever that might be,' said Mad Uncle Jack.

'Whatever that might be,' Eddie conceded, 'in America?'

'Spot-on, my boy! Spot-on!' cried Mad Uncle Jack. 'For years everything's run smoothly, and the editor has been in touch every six months with a report as to how the paper's been doing and a cheque for the profits to be shared between me and your father . . . except that we haven't heard from him of late, and we need someone to go from the family. Your father's bad back means that he can't go. Your mother's on crutches and, like your great-aunt, is also a woman, which leaves you or me, Edmund. I can't go, because I'm completely mad, so that leaves you. We want you to go to America as the representative of the Dickens family, to find out what's gone wrong in the offices of the *Terrible Times*.'

Eddie actually gasped out loud. What an adventure that would be!

Looking Backward, Looking Forward

In which we learn more of Eddie's past and more of his excitement at the upcoming voyage

When Eddie was very little, there was a fashion for sending boys to sea to toughen them up, particularly if they'd 'gone bad'. Eddie's parents had sent him to sea – in other words to work on a ship – not because he was a handful, but by mistake. They had meant to send a trunk, containing printing inks, to America by ship and Eddie to a school for extremely-young young gentlemen (him not being old enough to go to an ordinary school then). As it was, Eddie ended up on the vessel, and the trunk had a second-rate education for a boy, but a first-class education for a trunk. It sat at the back of the class and never said or did anything, which meant that it never did anything *wrong* and it didn't need feeding either, which made it very popular with the teachers. That trunk got better marks and end-of-term reports than the majority of the boys, so Eddie's parents were blissfully unaware that Eddie wasn't at the school (because it was a boarding school and he wasn't supposed to come home for the holidays either).

Eddie, meanwhile, grew up amongst sailors on a cargo ship. It was obvious to the sailors that Eddie wasn't a trunk – except for someone called the purser who said that if Eddie was down on the ship's inventory as a trunk then that's exactly what he was – but they were out at sea and they weren't going back just to put Eddie ashore. So Eddie spent his early years amongst the creaking rigging and was used to sleeping in a hammock, having the salty spray of the sea in his face and living off the toughest beef imaginable, which was packed in salt and stored in barrels. For some reason, it was full of maggots or weevils or maggots *and* weevils, but they added a bit of variety to the flavour as well as giving extra protein.

Eddie never reached America – the intended

destination for the now well-educated trunk – but he did learn to love a life on the ocean waves. He spent about eight years aboard ship in total and, by the end of it, could do some pretty impressive knots; could read a compass; had scrubbed the decks more hours than you've watched television in your entire life so far; and knew the workings of a ship from the tip of the main mast to the bilges below the waterline.

By one of those strange quirks of fate that God or Mother Nature throws up to show that He or She has a great sense of humour, Eddie finally landed back on English soil just as the trunk finished its schooling for extremely-young young gentlemen, and they both arrived back at home about the same time. Eddie was very excited and told his parents (who were pretty much strangers to him) about his exciting life on board ship. Being grown-ups, they only half-listened and, knowing full well that he'd actually been at school all this time, simply assumed that their only child had an overactive imagination.

They were puzzled by the trunk's return because they'd assumed it was lost at sea. Mr Brockenfeld, the editor of the *Terrible Times*, had sent a message saying that the inks had never arrived and now, all this time later, they'd somehow found their way back to their house (which later burnt down in the events outlined in *Awful End*).

One other side-effect of this strange mix-up was that, later in life, Eddie was to meet a few pupils of Glumberry School For Young Boys who assumed that they'd been at school with him – the trunk was always referred to as Edmund Dickens, remember – and were surprised how different he'd become.

'I remember you being much squarer shouldered when you were younger,' one Old Glumberry told him, for example.

A trip to America now, to try to find out what was going on at the *Terrible Times* offices, meant that Eddie would have a chance to re-acquaint himself with life at sea. (In those days, with the wind in your favour and no unexpected hitches or cock-ups, it took a clipper – a fast-sailing cargo ship – about two weeks to sail from England to the shores of North America. Steam ships were often slower, more expensive and, once in a while, blew up.) Eddie was really, really, *really* looking forward to it! He found an old atlas in Awful End's library and pored over it to try to work out the route the ship would be taking.

Eddie felt something jab him in the back. He turned to find that it was Malcolm the stuffed stoat's nose. Even Madder Aunt Maud had him

54

tucked under her arm. She was dressed in her nightclothes and her slippers were covered in snow which was melting on the library floor.

'What are you doing?' she demanded.

'Trying to see what route the ship will take that's carrying me to America,' he explained, holding up the huge atlas with enthusiasm.

'You're being carried to America?' asked Even Madder Aunt Maud.

'Not by a person,' Eddie explained. 'By ship.'

'We're on board ship?' asked Even Madder Aunt Maud, looking a little confused.

'No,' said Eddie. 'But I will be soon.'

'Then why lie to me?' his great-aunt demanded. 'I suppose you think it's clever to try to muddle an old lady?'

'I'm sorry if I didn't make myself clear,' said Eddie. 'I didn't mean to –'

Even Madder Aunt Maud raised Malcolm in the air by his tail. The meaning was obvious. It meant: *Silence, young man, or I might hit you over the head with this here stuffed stoat.*

'I don't like tricks,' she said. 'I haven't forgotten the time you dressed as a tree and jumped out at me!'

Eddie had certainly forgotten it. Or, to be more accurate, had no recollection of this event and rather suspected that (if it really had happened) it had been nothing to do with him.

'I don't think I've ever dressed as a tree, Even Madder Aunt Maud,' he protested.

'Exactly!' cried his great-aunt, her voice like someone drilling through a wall. 'You don't think! You don't think. Well, perhaps if you *did* think before you went and covered yourself in bark and leaves and jumped out on a poor old lady, then you wouldn't have done it.' She turned on her heels. 'Come, Malcolm,' she said, and left the library.

Eddie knew better than to try and protest his innocence any further, and went back to studying the atlas. After a while, he had the feeling that he was being watched, and looked around to see who, if anyone, was there. Framed in the doorway stood a complete stranger: a woman dressed in the finest of clothes.

'Master Dickens?' she enquired. (If you were that posh you didn't ask, you made enquiries.)

'Yes?' he said, politely.

'My name is Bustle, Lady Constance Bustle,' she said. 'Your father has asked me to act as your companion upon the upcoming voyage.'

Companion? It hadn't occurred to Eddie that his parents might worry about him travelling to America alone. It wasn't as if he wasn't used to a life at sea but, then again, there was still that confusion in his parents' minds.

'I'm delighted to meet you, Lady Constance,' said Eddie. She put out her gloved hand, and he strode across the library floor and kissed it. 'You've spoken to my father, you say?'

'Yes,' said Lady Constance. 'I've just come down from the scaffolding. He's currently painting an angel playing the harp, though I have to confess that, to me, it looks as if the angel is clutching an enormous vegetable and appears to be sitting on a large liver sausage.'

'That sounds like one of his clouds,' said Eddie.

'I suspected as much,' said Lady Constance. She had striking features (which doesn't mean that one wanted to hit her but that her face would stand out in a crowd, even though it would be a whopper to call her conventionally beautiful).

'My father isn't the world's greatest painter,' Eddie confessed. 'But he is most enthusiastic. What kind of vegetable, by the way?'

'A sprout,' said Lady Constance, 'though if it were that large in real life it would probably feed a family of four!' She laughed at her own joke in a snorty, horsy kind of way.

Eddie grinned. If he was going to have to have a companion on a long sea voyage, he could do worse than Lady Constance Bustle. Or so he thought.

'How did my father come to ask you to be my companion?' he asked. He'd never heard anyone mention her.

'I answered an advertisement,' she said. 'I was recently a companion to an elderly lady but she died.'

'I am sorry,' said Eddie, because that was the kind of thing you were expected to say when someone mentioned a death.

'I'm not,' replied Lady Constance. 'She was as sour as a bag of lemons . . . It was quite a relief when the railings on the edge of the ferry gave way and her bath chair tipped into the rapids.'

A bath chair's a kind of wheelchair. The one the old lady had been in was made of wicker. Her name had been Winifred Snafflebaum and her death caused quite a splash, both in the river and the local newspaper. The report said that Lady Constance had had to be restrained from jumping in after her employer to try to save her, though another eye-witness said that someone looking very like Lady Constance had brushed past him with a spanner in her hand not ten minutes before the ferry's railing had mysteriously 'given way'!

'So you're a companion by profession?' Eddie asked.

'Oh yes,' she nodded. 'Before the old lady, I was companion to a French woman. Sadly, she choked to death on a door handle.'

'How dreadful!' said Eddie.

'Most inconvenient,' Lady Constance agreed. 'I did so like living in Paris.'

'You must get to meet lots of different people,' said Eddie.

She nodded again. 'Though titled –' by which she meant being a 'lady', '– my family is a large one and the family fortune is small. In truth, it's not so much a fortune now as a large sock full of pennies under my father's bed. It has, therefore, been up to my eleven sisters and I to make our own way in the world. I could, of course, try to find some rich duke or baronet to marry, but I'd far rather travel the world as a companion. There's so much more freedom. It was simply bad luck that I was lumbered with such an objectionable old duck. She did leave me all her money though, which was nice.'

'I'm sure we'll have plenty of fun on the way to America and back,' said Eddie. He was a very well-mannered lad.

'There is one thing I should tell you whilst I remember,' said Lady Constance. 'I suffer from Dalton's Disease. Have you heard of it?'

Eddie had.

Dalton is probably famous for three things. Firstly, his Atomic Theory of 1808. In it, he claimed that if you kept cutting up something smaller and smaller and smaller you'd eventually come to something so small that it couldn't be cut up any more, and he called these smallest-of-small things atoms. Actually, he was wrong, because atoms can be cut up into sub-atomic particles and these can probably be broken up into sub-sub-atomic particles. Still awake? Excellent. But Dalton's Atomic Theory was *almost* right and way ahead of its time. It changed the way that everyone who thought about such things thought about such things, except for a small man in Alfriston, East Sussex, who stuck a finger in each ear and hummed loudly, stopping only occasionally only to shout: 'I'M NOT LISTENING!'

The second thing Dalton is famous for is keeping records of the local weather for just about every day of his adult life. Don't ask me why he did it. He just did. If he wanted to find out if it'd been raining in his back garden on a Wednesday twenty-five years previously, he could just look it up.

Thirdly, Dalton studied the problem he had with his vision. He was what we now call 'colour blind', and he did much to spread awareness of the condition. He even donated his eyeballs to science . . . for study *after* he died, of course. And that's why, in Eddie's day, colour-blindness was called Dalton's Disease. See? You pick up a book because of the funny picture on the cover and end up learning about some strange bloke who died in 1844. Isn't life just full of surprises?

Going . . . Going . . . ?

In which Eddie and the reader are almost halfway through the book and neither is sure whether he is ever going to get to America

The following Thursday, Mad Uncle Jack held a family meeting inside Marjorie the hollow cow. It was to have been in the library up at the main house, rather than inside a converted carnival float amongst the rose bushes, with onions hanging from the ceiling on strings, but Even Madder Aunt Maud had caught a cold from all that romping about in the snowdrifts after her shiny bauble, and was now in bed, and her husband had felt it important that she attend.

Also present were: Mad Uncle Jack himself, Mr and Mrs Dickens, their son Eddie, Lady Constance Bustle – who'd never been inside a hollow cow before – and Dawkins the gentleman's gentleman who was there to provide drinks . . . oh, and Malcolm, of course, if you count stuffed stoats. Jane, the failed chambermaid, was up in the house on her own, gibbering under the stairs, no doubt.

'This meeting is now in order!' Mad Uncle Jack announced, beating Even Madder Aunt Maud's bed with his dried swordfish for silence.

It hit her knees under the woolly blankets and she let out a cry: 'There's a dog on the bed! There's a dog on the bed!' Her cold had turned to a fever and she was slightly delirious. Make someone already as mad as Even Madder Aunt Maud *slightly* delirious and you get what by normal standards is *very* delirious.

'Where?' said MUJ, lifting the blankets to try to find the dog.

Eddie's father raised his hand, stiffly. 'Please ignore poor Aunt Maud, Uncle,' he said. 'And let's get on with the meeting, shall we?'

'What? Er, oh yes . . .' said MUJ. 'I wanted us to discuss plans for Eddie's voyage to America and visit to the offices of the *Terrible Times*. I'd like you to meet Eddie's travelling companion Lady Constance Bustle.'

Lady Constance stepped forward, parting the onions-on-strings above her head, as though pushing aside the leaves of an overhanging branch. 'I'm delighted to meet you all,' she said.

Even Madder Aunt Maud sat bolt upright in bed. 'You're pug ugly!' she gasped, which is another way of describing someone with striking or memorable features; a pug being a not-so-handsome breed of dog.

'Forgive my wife,' laughed Mad Uncle Jack. 'She's inclined to say what she thinks.'

Lady Constance wasn't sure what to say to *that*.

'A walking pair of nostrils!' cackled Even Madder Aunt Maud.

Mr Dickens was positioned between his aunt in bed and Eddie's travelling companion. 'Enchanted to meet you, Lady Constance,' he said, trying to lean forward to kiss her gloved hand but missing the target.

'Stay back, lady!' cried Even Madder Aunt Maud, with a barely suppressed guffaw. 'You'll frighten the stoat!' She waved Malcolm high above her head.

'I'm so pleased to know that my boy will be in your capable hands,' said Eddie's mother, Mrs Dickens. When Maud had started saying those embarrassing things to the titled newcomer, Mrs Dickens had become agitated and comforted herself by filling her mouth with the nearest thing to hand – the tassel of Even Madder Aunt Maud's dressing-gown – so what she actually said was: 'Um thow pweed cha now vat my bow wiw be inyaw caypabuw ands.'

Eddie's father was well used to understanding his wife when she had a mouth full of ice-cubes shaped like famous generals or anti-panic pills or acorns, for example, but no one else had the slightest idea what she'd just said, the corner of EMAM's dressing-gown cord trailing from the edge of her mouth, like a half-eaten snake.

If Lady Constance Bustle wished that she was anywhere except inside a cow-shaped carnival float with a bunch of misfits, she hid it very well. Perhaps it was her good breeding. Perhaps it was something else.

'Lady Constance comes to me with impeccable references,' said Eddie's father. 'I'm sure if they hadn't all died, each and every one of her previous employers would have been reluctant to let her go.'

Her list of previous employers was, indeed, impressive. They included: Sir Adrian Carter, the author, who died during a visit to the Royal Zoological Gardens when Lady Constance slipped on a discarded banana skin and pushed him into the gorilla cage; the philosopher and forward-thinker John Knoxford John, who drowned in game soup during a visit to the famous Barnum Soup Factory when an apparently involuntary spasm in the leg, possibly brought on by the cooking fumes, caused Lady Constance to kick him off a viewing platform and into a giant vat; the Duchess of Underbridge, who fell to her death in her own home, unaware that Lady Constance had had the stairs removed that night 'for cleaning'. The list was a long one.

As well as being well-known or wealthy people, they all had something else in common. According to the letters and wills presented by the distraught Lady Constance after their untimely deaths, they all left their money – often small fortunes, sometimes not so small – to their devoted companion, Lady Constance. Oh yes, and there was one *other* thing they all had in common, judging from these letters and wills: surprisingly similar handwriting.

'I feel sure that Eddie is in safe hands,' said Mad Uncle Jack.

'Pug ugly hands!' cried Even Madder Aunt Maud from her bed.

'Should somebody fetch the doctor?' suggested Lady Constance.

'Should somebody fetch a bag for your head?' suggested Even Madder Aunt Maud, which would be considered rude even by today's standards but in Eddie's day such a comment would have been considered OUTRAGEOUS.

'I really must apologise for my husband's aunt's behaviour,' said Mrs Dickens. 'She's not a well woman.' If only life were that simple because, of course, what she actually said was: 'Oy weierwy muscht apowoguys faw mow hushbangs awunts beavyvaw. Sheech nowtta weow woomang.'

On the word 'woman', or 'woomang', the tassel of Even Madder Aunt Maud's dressing-gown shot out of Eddie's mum's mouth and hit Lady Constance slap bang/slam bam/full-square in her striking (and/or pug ugly) face.

Her ladyship snarled – yes *snarled* – like a cornered cat and hit Mrs Dickens across her face with her muffler.

Those of you wondering why Lady Constance was holding a car component designed to keep exhaust pipes from being too noisy have got the wrong end of the stick . . . It wasn't *that* kind of muffler, which some folk call 'silencers'. Let me turn the stick around the other way so that you can hold the right end. The kind of muffler Eddie's mother was hit with was a piece of fur sewn into an open-ended cylinder in which well-to-do ladies stuck a hand into either end to keep them warm.

This meant that Mrs Dickens wasn't actually hurt by Lady Constance's attack, but was deeply shocked by it. She'd been apologising to her for her husband's aunt's rudeness and the spitting out of the dressing-gown tassel had obviously been an accident. And what did she get by way of thanks? A literal as well as a metaphorical slap in the face with a muffler!

Matters were made worse by the fact that, in the dim light of Marjorie's insides, Even Madder Aunt Maud mistook Lady Constance Bustle's furry muffler for her own beloved stuffed stoat, Malcolm.

'How dare you treat my Malcolm in that way!' she protested, grabbing the nearest thing – which happened to be the *real* Malcolm, resting by her pillow – and used him to lash out at the next nearest thing . . . which, or I should say who, happened to be poor old Mad Uncle Jack. The victim of yet another attack from his wife, MUJ fell to the floor of the cow with a terrible yell.

Lady Constance, meanwhile, was apologising to Mrs Dickens. 'Do forgive my hitting you in the face,' she said. 'It was a reflex action by my right arm as a direct result of having been hit on the nose by the regurgitated dressing-gown cord. Hitting my nose is like pressing a button. My arm swipes out like a lever. I'm only glad that it was my muffler which hit you and not my *fist*.' She said the last word as though she had experience of just what damage her fist could do.

'We quite understand,' said Mr Dickens hurriedly. 'I'm only sorry that my wife spat at you first.'

Eddie, who was helping his poor winded great-uncle to his feet, studied Lady Constance with interest. He was beginning to suspect that there was much more to her than met the eye.

I can't actually tell you what part of Mad Uncle Jack got hit by Malcolm – it's far too rude – but suffice it to say that it hurt a great deal for a while, but he soon recovered and there was no real harm done. It did, however, put an end to the meeting so it was agreed that Lady Constance should stay the night at Awful End and that they discuss the trip the following morning.

Now it's time to sort out the smart readers (anyone sensible enough to be reading such an excellent book as this) from the *very* smart readers. If you were wondering how on Earth Mr Dickens was suddenly able to attend a meeting inside Marjorie when, just a few pages ago, he was spending all his time on his back at the top of a wooden scaffolding rig, you fall into the very smart category. If you didn't spot that, don't worry. I write such beautiful prose that you were probably so engrossed in marvelling at my storytelling skills that you didn't let something as insignificant as how someone got to be somewhere bother you. Well, it's no big mystery, so let me explain:

Mad Uncle Jack had thought it important that everyone attend the Eddie-going-to-America meeting, so Dawkins (the gentleman's gentleman) and Gibbering Jane (the failed chambermaid) had been sent up the scaffolding to lash Mr Dickens to a plank of wood and lower him down to the ground on a pulley usually reserved for the chamber pot. Once on the floor of the hall of Awful End he was tipped upright (still lashed to the plank) and tied to a porter's trolley – one of those two-wheeled trolleys with a high back that railway porters sometimes still use to carry luggage – and wheeled down the garden to the hollow cow. Even this was harder than it sounded. Dawkins did the wheeling whilst Gibbering Jane ran ahead, gibbering, with a coal shovel, clearing a path through the snow.

It had been lashed to a plank and a porter's trolley, parked in the upright but rigid position inside the cow, that Mr Dickens had conducted himself at the meeting as I just outlined. If you think this is ridiculous, I should remind you that, near the end of the 20th century there was a film/movie/flick/motion picture called *The Silence of the Lambs* based on a book of the same name written by Thomas  Harris. In the film (which I have seen) and possibly the book (which I haven't read) the baddy (played by a very well-respected Welsh-born actor) is, at one stage, wheeled around on a porter's trolley AND he's wearing a silly mask, and everyone took that very seriously; so you can understand why, in the oh-so-polite 19th century, Lady Constance Bustle was far too polite to giggle or to ask what was going on . . . and the others probably just accepted it as perfectly normal. We

71

are talking about the *Dickens* family, don't forget.

With the meeting now over, Mr Dickens was untied from the porter's trolley, winched back up the wooden scaffolding rig, untied from the plank, which was then slid out from under him, and left in his usual position, staring up at the ceiling. He was in the process of painting 'Joseph and his coat of many colours' which, the truth be told – I am informed by someone who saw it before it was painted over years later – looked more like 'a mutant melting rainbow with a head, and fingers like liver sausages'. See? Just about everything he painted on that ceiling sounds as if it had at least something sausagy about it!

Mad Uncle Jack retired to his tree house, still winded. Even Madder Aunt Maud drifted off to sleep in Marjorie, dreaming about a pair of giant nostrils, and Eddie and his mother had supper at the kitchen table.

'I made the soup myself,' said his mother.

'What is it?' asked Eddie, studying the contents of his bowl. It looked very clear, except for the odd tiny leaf and what might possibly have been a dead fly.

'I used ingredients I found in the garden,' she said proudly.

'I thought the ground was far too hard to dig up vegetables,' said Eddie. 'Frozen solid.' He tasted the soup. It was like drinking hot water.

'I used melted snow,' she said. 'Oh look.' She took something out of her mouth. 'Here's one of Private Gorey's brass buttons.' She put it on the edge of her plate like a prune stone.

Eddie let out one of his silent sighs. He wished he was in America already!

... Gone!

*In which, to everyone's amazement, including the
author's, Eddie actually sets sail for America*

In Eddie's mind, he had imagined saying
goodbye to his mother on a quayside and then
striding up a gangplank to a ship. When the time
came – and amazingly, it did come – only Mad
Uncle Jack accompanied him and Lady
Constance on his farewell trip, and the ship was
anchored at the mouth of an estuary in deeper
water. The only way to reach the ship was by
rowing boat and climbing up a rope ladder.

When Eddie first met Mad Uncle Jack, he – Uncle Jack – used to go just about everywhere by horse (inside and out). But then, following Eddie's escape from an orphanage his horse bolted at the first sight of a giant hollow cow, whom we now know as Marjorie. When the poor frightened creature finally let itself be caught, it was a changed animal. Whereas before it was happy to do just about anything Mad Uncle Jack asked of it, now it dug its hooves in (which is, I suppose, the horsy equivalent of 'put its foot down') and regularly refused to gallop upstairs or jump over chimney sweeps . . . so MUJ spent much more time on foot.

He had acquired a new horse at the same time; Marjorie having been pulled along by one belonging to Mr and Mrs Cruel-Streak who'd run the St Horrid's Home for Grateful Orphans, from which Eddie (and the orphans) had escaped. Now it was obvious that the Cruel-Streaks cared more for their horse than the orphans in their so-called 'care', but the Dickenses were in no mood to return the animal to such nasty owners, so they kept him. Technically, this was theft but, as someone jolly famous was to announce a number of years later: all property is theft. (Wow! Think about that . . . You don't have to agree with it. Just think about it!)

This particular horse (whom they named

Edgar) was so used to being pampered that he spent much of his time sipping a small glass of sherry, reading *Bradfield's Horse & Hounds*. (The horse read *Bradfield's Horse & Hounds*, not the sherry. Sherry can't read. Come to think of it . . .)

Rather than travelling by pony and trap or horse and carriage, therefore, Mad Uncle Jack, Eddie and Lady Constance had travelled to the port by train.

Trains were at their most exciting back then. Locomotives made brilliant noises and belched out great billows of smoke from their gleaming funnels, and next to the driver on the open footplate stood the fireman, frantically stoking the furnace with fuel to create the steam to power the engine to turn the wheels.

Possibly the most famous engine driver of the steam-train era was the American Casey Jones. There are songs about him, a railway-station-based chain of burger outlets was named after him and there was even a long-running TV series about him and his heroic deeds . . . which is a bit strange when you realise that, in real life, he crashed his train, 'the old 638', and was killed in a terrible accident which was, according to the official investigation at the time, entirely his fault 'as a consequence of not having properly responded to flag signals'. Weird, huh? But I digress. Back to Eddie's train:

As well as first- and second-class carriages there were third-class ones too, which were usually jam-packed full of slightly grubby people carrying bulging sacks or live chickens. They may not have started out the journey grubby, but – jam-packed with all those other people – they always ended it that way. Some third-class passengers also ended up with chickens they hadn't set off with. Such people are technically known as 'thieves'.

MUJ, Eddie and Lady Constance were in the first-class carriages, which were very different. In the first-class dining car, pink flamingos stood on one leg each in an ornamental pond with plush velvet seats neatly arranged around it in semicircles. The windows in first class had shutters, blinds *and* curtains – whereas in third class they relied on the grime to keep out the light, when travelling at night – and all the fixtures and fittings were either made of gleaming metal or highly polished wood. In fact the insides of the first-class carriage and dining car were probably a lot nicer than most people's homes!

Eddie's travelling trunk was far too big to fit in the train carriage, let alone put on a rack, so it had been loaded into the guard's van. Eddie, however, was not so lucky. Mad Uncle Jack insisted that he spend much of the journey lying in one of the luggage racks above the seats.

'It's to get you used to life at sea, m'boy!' he explained. 'They don't have beds on board ship, you know, they have hummocks.'

'Hammocks,' Eddie corrected him. (Hummocks are very small hills.) He'd tried to tell Mad Uncle Jack that he'd had plenty of experience of life on the ocean waves and couldn't he please sit in a seat like anyone else . . . but failed.

The luggage rack was uncomfortable enough as it was but when Lady Constance stuck her parasol – a small umbrella designed to keep off the sun rather than the rain – up there alongside him, it was really uncomfortable . . . but nothing could dampen his excitement of going to America to find out what had gone wrong at the offices of the *Terrible Times*.

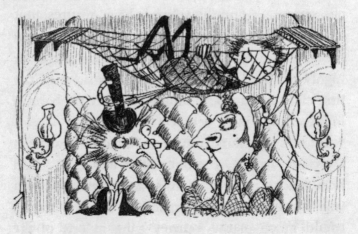

When they finally reached the port and Mad Uncle Jack lifted Eddie off the luggage rack, the poor boy had mesh-marks all over his clothes and bare arms.

'It suits you,' whispered Lady Constance.

Eddie grinned. O, foolish, foolish child. (I'm allowed to say things like that because I know what's going to happen later.)

Somehow a porter managed to wheel Eddie's huge trunk, with Lady Constance's bags balanced precariously on top, out of the busy station, with one single journey of a porter's trolley. It was similar to the one that Dawkins and Gibbering Jane had used to transport Eddie's father to and from Marjorie. They passed a ragbag of street vendors trying to sell everything from newspapers and fresh(-ish) fruit to quack remedies (which are not cures for quacking but so-called cures that didn't really offer any relief except, of course, relieving you of your money to pay for them). Mad Uncle Jack hailed a cab in his own inimitable way. He rummaged in his coat and, producing a large dried puffer fish from his pocket, he threw it with all his might at a passing cab-driver; knocking the poor man's hat clean off.

'Strewth!' said the cabbie, swerving his cab in the direction the projectile had been thrown. I think I'd have said a lot worse if the dried puffer fish had hit me. The puffer fish gets its name from puffing out into a big spiky ball, and note the adjective 'spiky'. A dried one of those thrown at your head could cause quite an 'OUCH!!!'

'Who threw that?' demanded the enraged driver.

'It was me,' said Mad Uncle Jack. 'You can keep the change.' To those who knew him, this made complete sense. He 'paid' for everything with dried fish and, by his reckoning, a puffer fish was quite high currency (more of a twenty-pound note than nickel and dime change). Of course, those who knew him also knew to parcel up the fish and send them to Eddie's father, Mr Dickens, who then sent them actual money in exchange. Those who didn't know Mad Uncle Jack and his unusual ways thought that he was either someone trying to make a fool out of them, or that he was a nutter. Or both. Which was exactly what the angry cabbie was thinking as he charged horse and cab towards the kerb.

'Do you take me for some kind of a fool?' he demanded.

'I take you to be a cab driver waiting for a fare and we are a fare waiting for a cab-driver,' said MUJ, blissfully unaware that he'd caused minor injury and major offence. (A 'fare' not only meant payment but also a passenger in the cab.) He patted the cabbie's horse.

While Mad Uncle Jack and the cab driver were talking – you can't really call it an argument because it takes two to argue – Eddie opened a door of the cab and Lady Constance stepped inside and sat down. Next Eddie stepped in and sat down beside her. With more strength than his stick-like body suggested was possible, Mad Uncle Jack helped the porter heave the heavy trunk off the porter's trolley and on to the roof of the cab, then threw Lady Constance's luggage up after it, piece by piece.

The cabbie knew he was beaten and let the thin, beaky man climb inside the cab without further fuss or delay. 'Where to, guv'nor?' he asked, which is what they still teach cab-drivers to say at cab-driving school today.

'To the *Pompous Pig*,' said MUJ. 'She's due to set sail today.'

'To America,' Eddie added excitedly.

'Aha!' said the cabbie, obviously pleased to know something they didn't. 'She's too big to dock in the port in this tide, so they've dropped anchor at the river's mouth. You'll have to get a boat out to it from Muddy Straits. I'll take you there.' He swished his horse's reins and they were off.

'Muddy Straits sounds rather *muddy*,' Eddie called out.

'It did indeed get its name on account of the

mud,' said the cabbie, knowledgeably.

Muddy Straits was a large area of grey, damp mud which birdwatchers so love and which the rest of us find so boring that you're almost guaranteed that nowadays it would be turned into an area of Special Scientific Interest, with its own leaflet explaining why it was important not to turn this boggy habitat into a new four-runway airport. The snow had long since melted, so the mud was there in all its glory, for all to see.

'It's a shame this mud can't be put to some good use,' said Mad Uncle Jack when he stepped out of the cab and took in his surroundings. 'Put in a brightly coloured fancy package, with a pretty bow on top, and I'm sure it would appeal to ladies.'

'But what would they use it for?' asked Eddie, who had paid the driver with real money – he'd been given some for the voyage – before the whole payment-with-fish approach could rear its ugly head and upset the poor man again. The luggage was then heaved to the ground.

'What do ladies *do* with half the things they own: china ornaments, trinkets, mementoes? They leave them cluttering up the place, that's what they do. Little packets of mud needn't be different. They don't have to be *for* anything.'

'The skin,' said Lady Constance, dusting the top of the trunk with a handkerchief, removed from her sleeve, before sitting down upon it and rearranging her dress.

'I beg your pardon?' said Eddie.

'The skin,' said Lady Constance. 'Some types of mud are said to be particularly good for the skin. Ladies have been known to wear mud packs upon their faces. There are even some in society who believe a mud bath to be most revivifying.'

Eddie hadn't the foggiest what 'revivifying' meant, but he didn't much like the idea of having a bath in mud . . . Well, certainly not in the mud around Muddy Straits. It looked gloopy and smelly, with tufts of marshy weeds sprouting out in places, reminding him of the nostril hairs Even Madder Aunt Maud had trimmed from the nose of her stuffed stoat.

'I cannot imagine my beloved,' (which is pronounced as though spelled belove-ed, as in the name 'Ed' short for Eddie, short for Edmund) 'wearing a mud pack upon her face!' said Mad Uncle Jack in obvious amazement.

Eddie could imagine quite the opposite. If anyone was mad enough to smear mud all over her face, then Even Madder Aunt Maud was the one!

'Poor Mrs Riversedge,' (which is spelled like 'rivers edge' but pronounced 'river sedge') 'suffocated whilst wearing a homemade mud pack

I had prepared,' said Lady Constance.

'One of your employers?' asked Eddie.

Lady Constance nodded, wiping a non-existent tear from her eye. 'I'm afraid so.'

The cabbie, meanwhile, had raised his hat and left them at the water's edge. It was only when he'd clattered off with his cab that it occurred to MUJ that he'd need a ride back to the railway station once he'd seen off his great-nephew and the boy's travelling companion on the *Pompous Pig*.

'Now what?' asked Eddie. 'Are we supposed to swim out to the boat?'

'Ship,' said Lady Constance.

'I beg your pardon?' said Eddie.

'It's a ship, not a boat,' said Lady Constance.

'What's the difference?' asked Eddie.

For all I know, Lady Constance was about to reply 'about three points in Scrabble with the letters on ordinary squares' – except, of course, Scrabble hadn't been invented back then – because she never got to tell Eddie the difference. They were interrupted by a loud whistle.

'Look!' said Mad Uncle Jack, pointing excitedly at a sparrow passing them overhead. 'An albatross!' He never was very good at identifying wildlife and once mistook a badger for a lance-corporal in his regiment. 'I'd recognise that cry anywhere!'

'Er, that was a whistle,' said Eddie.

'Coming from that rowing boat,' said Lady Constance pointing at the little boat heading for them.

The oarsman reached the shallows and jumped out into the water, his feet protected by a pair of high leather boots. He dragged the boat behind him.

'Lady Constance Bustle and Master Edmund Dickens?' he asked, in that 'oo-arr' accent which sailors always seem to have in pirate stories.

'Yes,' said Eddie excitedly.

'Indeed,' nodded Lady Constance.

'I'm Jolly,' said the sailor.

'I'm somewhat cheerful myself,' said Eddie's great-uncle, 'despite most of my family being ill or injured.'

'You misunderstand, sir,' said the sailor. 'My name be Jolly.'

'Aha!' nodded Mad Uncle Jack. 'You're Mr B Jolly . . . What does the "B" stand for? Brian?'

'No sir, you see –'

'Benjamin?'

'No, I –'

'Benedict? Bernard? Balthazar?'

'I –'

'Bill?'

'No, my –'

'No, if you were Bill your initial would be "W" and not "B" because your first name would be William –'

'ROGER!' shouted the sailor in desperation.

'I beg your pardon?' said Mad Uncle Jack.

'My name, sir . . . My name be Roger but me shipmates call me Jolly.'

'I see,' said Eddie with glee. 'Because the skull-and-crossbones flag is called the Jolly Roger!'

'That be right, young gentleman!' said the sailor with a toothless grin.

'I do hope the *Pompous Pig* isn't a pirate vessel!' said Lady Constance.

'I wouldn't let Captain Skrimshank hear you speak like that, m'lady,' said Jolly. 'He prides himself on being one of Her Majesty's most loyal subjects. He carries a picture of her with him everywhere.'

'I, on the other hand,' said Mad Uncle Jack, 'carry portraits of my own family with me everywhere.' He opened his long checked coat to reveal a series of small oil paintings somehow fixed to the lining, the tail of the dried swordfish he used as an ear-cleaner-cum-back-scratcher sticking from an inner pocket. Eddie had first laid eyes on these pictures when his great-uncle had nailed them up on a visit to his house, since destroyed by fire.

Jolly eyed the oil paintings. He eyed the tail of the dried fish. He eyed Mad Uncle Jack. 'I think we'd better be gettin' to the *Pompous Pig*,' he said. Then he eyed the large trunk. 'That'll leave us low in the water.' Soon they, and their luggage, were in the rowing boat.

The goodbyes were brief and, in next to no time, Mad Uncle Jack was just a small dot in the distance. Soon Eddie was stepping off the boat and climbing up the rope ladder after Lady Constance, to find himself on the deck of the ship that was intended to carry them to foreign shores.

*

Unlike his many years at sea 'below decks', Eddie now had a proper cabin to himself, connected by an inner 'adjoining door' to Lady Constance's. He had a proper bed, too, not the hammock (nor, to be more accurately inaccurate, the hummock) MUJ had predicted.

According to the first mate, Mr Spartacus Briggs, who had greeted them and shown them around the ship on their arrival, there was only one other paying passenger on board, but Eddie had yet to meet him. This was not a pleasure cruise, nor a ship full of immigrants wanting to start a new life in the fairly new (but not quite so new as it used to be) New World of the Americas. It was, first and foremost, a merchant vessel taking cargo to America, with the intention of filling up with other goods in America and bringing them home to Britain. The paying passengers were an added source of income – more money, money, money – for the ship's owners.

When Eddie did finally lay eyes on their fellow passenger he couldn't believe them. A feeling of horror, which started at his heels and spread all over his body like a hot flush, soon engulfed him. It couldn't be . . . surely?

But it was.

There on the deck stood a man he'd last seen in an arrowed suit, with a ball and chain fitted to his ankle. It was the escaped convict Swags.

The man's hooded eyes met his with a piercing stare. There was no doubt in Eddie's mind that the villain recognised him in return. It was unlikely that Swags would have forgotten him. Eddie had helped in the capture of one of his fellow convicts – the leader of his little group, in fact – which probably made him not only memorable but *very unpopular*, too!

What made matters even worse, of course, was that, on board ship, there was nowhere to run . . .

Episode 8

Discoveries

In which Eddie may be at sea, but we seem to spend most of the time amongst familiar faces on dry land

How Even Madder Aunt Maud came to be in Eddie's large sea trunk no one knows to this day. It became a regular topic of conversation in the Dickens family and many theories have been put forward over the years, even from Dickenses who weren't even born at the time, but the truth went with Even Madder Aunt Maud to her grave – buried inside Marjorie in her beloved rose garden – not long after her 126th birthday (which is nearly a quarter of a century after Eddie, Lady Constance and Maud-in-the-trunk set sail for America).

What *is* known is that it took nearly a week at sea before Even Madder Aunt Maud was discovered aboard the *Pompous Pig*, because she soon vacated the trunk and moved about the ship, sleeping in a variety of places from the cook's cauldron in the galley to the crow's nest at the top of the main mast.

There had been rumours spreading around the ship of a strange being cackling to herself and taking things but Eddie knew from experience that sailors were a superstitious bunch who drank a lot, which didn't make them the best eye-witnesses when apparently 'seeing things'. It was only when Eddie heard a number of reports of this apparition – variously described as a 'water witch' and 'sea hag' and everything in between – wielding some kind of animal, possibly a rigid ferret, that Eddie began to fear the worst; that his great-aunt and Malcolm had somehow got on board!

It took almost as long for the folks back at Awful End to discover that Even Madder Aunt Maud had gone missing. With Mr Dickens up his wooden scaffolding rig, Gibbering Jane under the stairs, Mad Uncle Jack back in his tree house, Mrs Dickens pootling about doing whatever she did and poor old Dawkins, the gentleman's gentleman, doing everyone's bidding, they probably assumed that Even Madder Aunt Maud was in Marjorie or, on finding the cow empty, had just nipped out with Malcolm for a breath of fresh air. When they did finally realise that she was well and truly GONE, they had no idea where. There were no telephones, no ship-to-shore telegraphs or radios, and the word 'email' was nothing more than a misspelling of 'female', with the 'f' missing; so there was no way that those aboard the *Pompous Pig* could let them know she was safe and well. To put it bluntly, the folk at Awful End were baffled. She seemed to have vanished into thin air.

MUJ went to the local police station to report his wife missing. He knew the detective inspector from a previous encounter and demanded to see him. Knowing that Mad Uncle Jack was the gentleman living up at 'the big house' and completely mad, of course, the sergeant at the front desk led him straight through to the inspector's office. The front desk was a new idea and the sergeant was still in the looking-at-it-admiringly stage, and was keen to get back to it. He'd bought a tin of beeswax with his own money (and he didn't get paid very much so this was beyond the call of duty). He intended to wax and polish the front desk in his lunch hour which was, for some inexplicable reason, only 45 minutes long.

'There's this madman to see you, sir,' said the

sergeant, showing MUJ into the inspector's office. The inspector was sitting behind his desk on a pile of gazetteers (which are a kind of book). He was a very large man and his desk chair had recently broken under the weight of him. The detective inspector struggled to his feet. 'Ah, Mad Mr Dickens,' he said in greeting. 'How may I be of service?'

Mad Uncle Jack fumbled in his pocket and pulled out a dried halibut. A halibut is a flat fish and therefore, if you're that way inclined, an ideal fish to write on. 'My wife has disappeared,' he explained. 'I've made some notes on her last known movements.'

'Disappeared, you say?' said the detective inspector.

'Disappeared,' MUJ nodded. He handed the policeman the dried halibut.

The inspector could not read so did not know that MUJ's scribbles were writing. He simply assumed that the dried fish had strange markings and was being proffered as a snack – in much the same way that you or I might offer someone a crisp/potato chip – so he tried to take a bite out of it. He nearly broke his teeth.

'What are you doing?' demanded Mad Uncle Jack, wanting to know why the detective was eating his carefully written notes.

'What are *you* doing?' demanded the inspector, wanting to know why on Earth he had been handed an uneatable snack. (And, no, the word shouldn't be 'inedible'. If something's inedible, it means that you can physically eat it but it's so horrible that no one in their right mind would want to. If something's uneatable, you physically can't eat it; such as a chunk of rock . . . or one of Mad Uncle Jack's dried fish.)

'I want you to read my notes!' Mad Uncle Jack protested. He had been around to every member of the household asking them when they'd last actually seen Even Madder Aunt Maud and had carefully written down their responses. Now he could see that there were teeth marks on his notes and that the detective's saliva had smudged some of the replies . . . and he'd been very proud of his initial investigations!

The inspector was equally angry. 'I may not be able to read,' he said, 'but I know the difference between a piece of paper and a dried fish, and I don't take kindly to you trying to make a fool out of me!'

'Can't read?' spluttered Mad Uncle Jack. 'Who ever heard of a police inspector who can't read?'

'Me for one, sir,' said the sergeant from the front desk who'd come back into the office to ask to borrow a cloth for the polishing. 'The detective inspector, here, can't read and he's the best detective inspector for miles around.'

'Thank you, Sergeant,' said the inspector, returning to his seat of books and sitting back down behind his desk.

'I expect you're the ONLY detective inspector for miles around!' said the clearly agitated Mad Uncle Jack.

'Not true!' said the inspector and was about to pull out a map marked with the county's police stations when he thought better of it. He placed the dried halibut on his desk and then folded his arms across his stomach. 'Do, please, sit down, Mad Mr Dickens, and tell me all about your dear lady wife's disappearance.'

The detective inspector may not have been able to read but he was certainly a very good detective inspector. He listened very carefully to what MUJ had to say and, based on the facts laid out before him, made an initial hypothesis (not to be confused with an initialled hippopotamus . . . which is rather unlikely, come to think of it).

'It would seem that no one has seen your wife since you, your great-nephew Edmund and his travelling companion Lady Constance left to catch the *Pompous Pig*,' said the inspector, 'which leads me to conclude that she either disappeared during your brief absence or, somehow, went with you.'

'How do you mean went with us?' asked Mad Uncle Jack, so deep in concentration that he was unaware that he was combing his moustache with the serrated edge of his dried swordfish's nose.

'That she hung on to the back or underside of your coach, or somehow got inside your great-nephew's luggage,' said the police officer, which would have sounded crazy if they weren't talking about Even Madder Aunt Maud. He'd met her once before and had built up an extremely accurate psychological profile of her: completely bonkers.

'Well . . .' said Mad Uncle Jack, a little

hesitantly, 'I suppose that's a possibility. In our early years of marriage, she did once glue herself to the underside of a performing African elephant when the circus came to town, so went with them to the next venue, though she did reassure me afterwards that it'd been by mistake . . . She's a truly remarkable woman.'

'Remarkable,' repeated the inspector, as he was prone to do; though he said the word as though it wasn't necessarily the one he'd have chosen first and foremost to describe Mad Uncle Jack's missing spouse.

'And what about the other possibility? Her disappearing during my absence instead?' asked MUJ, slipping the dried fish back into his pocket.

'That would be more of a coincidence,' the detective pointed out, 'but not an impossibility. If she'd disappeared during the period when there were all those breakouts from Grimpen Jail and escaped convicts on the loose, I'd be concerned for her safety. But all the escapees, bar one, were recaptured a long, long time ago and the single one still at large will have fled the district long ago, too. No, in my professional opinion, your wife has probably ended up aboard the *Pompous Pig*.'

'If she was simply hanging on to the back or underside of our carriage, she might have dropped off at the station before we got on the train,' Mad Uncle Jack pointed out.

'If that was the case, she, or someone who ran into her, would have probably been in contact with you by now,' the inspector reasoned. 'She has a . . . er, very distinctive way about her.' What he actually meant was that a potty woman wielding a stuffed stoat would stick out like a pyramid in a sandpit.

'But what makes you so sure that she's actually aboard my great-nephew's ship?' asked Mad Uncle Jack.

'The very fact that there's been no report of anyone having seen her,' said the detective inspector. 'If she's on the *Pompous Pig*, neither she nor the crew can contact us unless they land and send someone ashore with a message . . . and the first stop after Ireland is America itself.' He struggled to his feet once more. 'Just to be doubly sure, I'll have my sergeant check the daily reports from other districts to see whether there have been any sightings, but I'm sure I'd have remembered them from the morning briefings. I'll also have him fill in a full missing person's report. I have all the information I need stored in here.' He tapped the side of his head and a small, round peppermint fell out of his ear on the opposite side, and rolled across the floor.

The policeman was more startled than Mad Uncle Jack, who simply assumed that the detective inspector had a head full of them. What had actually happened was that the inspector'd had a peppermint in his hand before dozing off at his desk, resting his head in said hand. The peppermint had got pushed into his ear and, when he'd been awoken by the sergeant knocking at the door to his office, he'd sat bolt upright, blissfully unaware that the peppermint had been lodged there . . . until now.

'If you find anything out, please inform me immediately,' said Mad Uncle Jack. 'You can usually find me in my tree house.'

'If *you* find anything out, please inform *me* immediately,' added the detective inspector. 'You can usually find me in *my* tree house.'

'You have a tree house?' asked Mad Uncle Jack.

'No,' confessed the detective inspector. 'I don't

know what made me say that. Sorry.'

Mad Uncle Jack left the police station, striding past the desk sergeant who was watching the hands of the police station clock approach the hour. He was itching to get out his beeswax and make a start on his desk.

Episode 9

That Sinking Feeling

In which both Eddie and Mad Uncle Jack make plans regarding the 'recapture' of Even Madder Aunt Maud

The first thing Eddie did on seeing Swags, the escaped convict on board the *Pompous Pig*, was to tell Lady Constance.

'Are you sure that it's him?' she asked when he'd told her the whole story.

'I'm sure,' nodded Eddie, wishing that there was some room for doubt.

'And is Swags his real name?'

He thought hard. 'I think it was short for Swagman, but that was only a nickname, too.'

'I believe that a swagman is an Australian drifter,' said Lady Constance, with a puzzled frown.

'That's it!' said Eddie. 'I remember now. He was given the nickname because he'd been sent on a convict ship to Australia but had somehow escaped back to England . . . only to be jailed for something else and to escape again. This time to the moors.'

'And it looks like he's now trying to escape to America,' said Lady Constance, letting it sink in.

'So what should we do? Inform the captain?' asked Eddie. 'He could be dangerous.'

'Do you know what Swags was in jail for?' asked his travelling companion.

'No,' Eddie confessed.

'So he could be harmless,' said Lady Constance. 'I've heard stories of men being convicted for stealing a loaf of bread, and I don't think a loaf-thief will do much harm . . .'

'He might do if he's afraid of being caught!' protested Eddie. 'And, anyway, for all we know, Swag could be a murderer!'

They were in Eddie's cabin, him sitting on his bed and Lady Constance in a chair. She stood up and sat down next to him on the bed, taking his hand. 'Eddie,' she said. 'You don't even know his real name. You don't know what he was originally locked up for and it's your word against his that he's an escaped convict. Don't you think it would be better to say nothing?'

'I . . . I . . .' Eddie was speechless. This wasn't what he'd expected her to say at all.

'Not only that, he's unlikely to try to harm you if he wants to get to America, isn't he? It's in his best interest to behave himself and to keep a low profile. If he goes around threatening people he'll simply draw attention to himself but, if he does try anything, then we should go straight to Mr Briggs or Captain Skrimshank. Agreed?' asked Lady Constance.

'Agreed,' sighed Eddie but, in his heart of hearts, he wanted to inform the captain right then.

*

When Eddie later told Lady Constance of his suspicions – his *conviction* – that Even Madder Aunt Maud had somehow got on board the ship, her reaction was completely different.

'We must warn . . . er, that is *tell* Mr Briggs at once. We must find your poor great-aunt before she harms herself or, possibly, the *Pompous Pig*. Who knows what she and that stuffed stoat of hers might get up to unchecked!'

They hurried off together to find the first mate.

He was on the smaller upper deck, where the huge steering wheel thingy was – I don't know the nautical term – standing by a scruffy young boy who was actually 'at the wheel', steering the vessel.

'We have reason to believe that there's a stowaway on board,' said Lady Constance, whom Eddie noticed was fluttering her eyebrows at the handsome Mr Spartacus Briggs in a way he'd never seen her flutter them in front of anyone else.

'Really, Lady Constance?' asked the first mate, straightening himself to his full height in his fine uniform. 'Do you have any idea who it is?'

'Young Master Edmund's great-aunt,' said Lady Constance.

The boy – for he was no more than that – at the wheel smirked at Eddie. He was in a tattered sailor suit and had gaps in his teeth. He reminded Eddie of the orphans he'd helped escape from St Horrid's a while back.

Mr Briggs looked disappointed. 'Your great-aunt?' he said, turning his attention to Eddie.

'I'm afraid so, Mr Briggs,' he said. The first mate had insisted, at their first meeting, that it would be wrong to call him 'sir'. 'She's the sea witch with the ferret your men have been reporting seeing . . . only she's not a witch, just Even Madder Aunt Maud, and it's not a ferret but her stuffed stoat Malcolm.'

'I see,' said Mr Spartacus Briggs, though he obviously didn't. It was hard for Eddie to explain his relatives to someone who'd not met them face to face. 'How do you think she got on board?'

'She must have been inside my trunk,' said Eddie. 'It was very heavy but, when I opened it after your men put it in my cabin, there was only an apple core and a single handkerchief inside.'

'And you didn't think to report it?' asked Mr Briggs. 'I mean, didn't you consider the possibility that say, for example, some of the men aboard this ship might have stolen its contents?'

'It was mainly clothes,' said Eddie, 'and, with the way things happen in my family, I assumed one of my relatives must simply have unpacked what I'd packed.'

'The Dickenses are a most unusual family,' Lady Constance added helpfully. 'Unique, I hope.'

Eddie wasn't listening. 'Now it's obvious that Even Madder Aunt Maud must have emptied the trunk and climbed inside.'

'But why would she want to be a stowaway on a ship to America?' pondered Mr Briggs.

'Oh, I doubt she planned anything like that,' said Eddie, surprised that the first mate should even consider that his great-aunt would have had anything sensible, like a plan! 'I expect she saw the trunk and thought it was a comfortable place to have a quick sleep, or some such thing.'

'I see,' said Mr Briggs. 'Er, I have just two more questions before I report this to the captain.'

'Yes?'

'Firstly, have you any idea how we might – er – get your great-aunt to come out into the open?'

'I'm sorry?' asked Eddie.

'He means do you have any thoughts on how they might capture her?' explained Lady Constance.

A big grin spread across Eddie's face. He'd just had a brilliant idea. It was obvious! Why hadn't he thought of it before? He needn't have involved the crew. 'Shiny things!' he cried. 'It's worked before and it'll work again. Shiny things!'

'Shiny fings?' asked the boy at the wheel.

'Quiet, Powder Monkey!' the first mate ordered. 'Concentrate on steering.'

'Yes, sir,' said the boy, looking down at the ship's wheel deck with a sheepish look on his face.

'Shiny things?' asked Mr Spartacus Briggs and Lady Constance Bustle as one.

Eddie nodded. 'My great-aunt's a bit like a jackdaw,' Eddie began.

'But your great-*uncle*'s the one with a nose like a beak,' said Lady Constance, which was another of her not-so-ladylike comments.

'I mean that she seems to love collecting shiny objects nowadays. Last summer there was a highly polished mortar shell . . . recently there was the crystal bauble from a chandelier . . . She can't resist them.'

'So if we were to bait a trap with a shiny object, we could lie in wait and – er – encourage her to stay in your cabin with you rather than frighten the men?' nodded Mr Briggs. 'I think we have the makings of a plan here, Master Dickens. Well done!'

'That's all very well, Mr Briggs,' said Eddie's travelling companion. 'But do you have anything particularly shiny on board?'

'There's always the sextant,' said Mr Briggs.

'The what?' asked Lady Constance.

'It's the instrument used for calculating latitude, by working out the angle of the sun from the horizon,' said Eddie, to their amazement. 'It's often made of polished brass.' (This boy had been to sea before, remember.)

'Exactly!' said Mr Briggs. He slapped Eddie on the back. 'Well done, lad.' Eddie only just managed to stop himself falling to the deck. That was some slap!

'Sorry to spoil the party,' said Lady Constance, 'but you must have been using your sextant throughout the voyage already.'

'And?' asked Mr Briggs.

'It ain't attracted the dotty old lady yet, so why should it now?' said Powder Monkey, getting a thwack around the ear for his trouble.

'Back down to the galley with you!' ordered the first mate, but he didn't look too angry. Powder Monkey scurried off between their legs and Mr Briggs took the wheel.

'He seems rather young to be steering this ship,' said Lady Constance.

Mr Briggs smiled. 'He's really a galley hand – a kitchen helper – but he's a good lad and has been pestering me to show him the ropes.'

'You're a kind man,' said Lady Constance, fluttering those eyelashes of hers again.

'You have a good point about the sextant,' said

Eddie. 'We'll have to think of something really shiny to bring Even Madder Aunt Maud out of hiding.'

With one hand on the wheel, and his eyes on the horizon – not literally, of course, or they'd have to be on very long stalks – the first mate rubbed his chin, deep in thought. 'I can think of just the thing to attract her,' he said. 'The shiniest of shiny things. It can't fail . . . but I must talk with Captain Skrimshank first.'

'Excellent!' said Lady Constance.

'What was your second question?' asked Eddie.

'I beg your pardon?'

'You originally said you had two questions for me, Mr Briggs.'

'Ah, yes,' said the first mate. 'I was wondering why you didn't have any clothes on?'

Of course Eddie wasn't *naked* naked, he was *almost* naked – he was in his undies – but that was still a very odd way for a paying passenger (back then) to be wandering around a ship.

'As I said, Mr Briggs, all my clothes were missing from my trunk. I've only got the ones I came aboard with and Lady Constance has kindly washed those because they were beginning to . . . to . . .'

'Smell a little ripe,' said his professional companion, finding the right words. 'They're currently drying in the rigging.' She nodded in the

109

direction of one of the masts where, sure enough, Eddie's clothes were tied to a rope like flags, fluttering in the breeze.

'Remarkable,' said Mr Briggs. 'Truly remarkable. Now, if you will excuse me, I shall have Jolly take the wheel and will consult the captain about our plan.'

Despite his various aches and pains from attacks with a toasting fork and a stuffed stoat, Mad Uncle Jack somehow made it to the top of his nephew's wooden scaffolding rig, in the hallway of Awful End. Eddie's father was, of course, lying at the top, busy painting something which looked suspiciously like – you guessed it – a liver sausage.

'We have to get her back,' said Mad Uncle Jack. 'I can't live without her for that long, you know.'

'I know,' said Mr Dickens.

'She may live in a hollow cow and me in my tree

house,' MUJ continued, 'but we're always in the same vicinity. She is my love, my joy, my reason for living . . . I cannot bear to be away from her grating voice and violent attacks.'

'I quite understand,' said Mr Dickens, wiping his paintbrush on a stained rag before dabbing it in a different colour on the palette that lay on his chest. 'But what if the detective inspector is wrong, Mad Uncle Jack? What if Even Madder Aunt Maud isn't on board the *Pompous Pig* but riding the trains up and down the line, or living on wild berries up on the moors? She was very taken with the place after we all crash-landed there in that hot-air balloon, remember?'

This would be an excellent place for me to go on about one of my earlier books again, but I'm writing this part on a Sunday and it somehow doesn't feel right . . . but perhaps Suzy, my editor, will read it on a weekday and say: 'Go on! Mention the title. It'd be a waste not to!' We'll just have to wait and see.

'I cannot take the risk that my darling love-pumpkin is aboard the *Pompous Pig* with young Edmund and do nothing about it,' said Mad Uncle Jack. He was distracted for a moment by something Eddie's father had finished painting on the ceiling the day before. To any sane person, what it most resembled was a large marrow, or

111

some such vegetable, with arms and legs, clutching a large – yup – liver sausage. 'Moses holding the Ten Commandments?' he asked.

'Yes,' Mr Dickens beamed with pride.

'Such delicate brushwork!' said Mad Uncle Jack. 'Breathtaking!' He began to wheeze.

'But how can anyone hope to catch up with Simon's ship?' asked Mr Dickens. By Simon he, of course, meant his son Eddie. 'They have over a week's start on us.'

'I have a plan!' said Mad Uncle Jack dramatically throwing his arms wide which, in his crouched position, caused him to topple off the edge of the scaffolding.

Gibbering Jane emerged from under the stairs, with a sinking feeling, to find out what had caused the nasty 'CRUNCH'.

Episode 10

Dazzling Events

In which not only Even Madder Aunt Maud shows
an interest in a priceless shiny thing

Later that same day, Eddie and Lady Constance were taken to the captain's cabin. In fact, Captain Skrimshank had a suite of rooms, including the dining room where Eddie and Lady Constance ate their evening meals with the captain and first mate, served by the steward.

They'd only been in this room once before, though, and that had been when they had first been introduced to Skrimshank. It was like an office, with a big table laid out with charts, a compass on some kind of gyroscope so that it was always level, even when the ship listed (which is nautical/maritime/sailor-speak for tilted or rocked about), and various other brass implements from a magnifying glass to a pair of dividers. There were books on shelves on the walls and a small safe in the corner, by the door. Behind the captain and his table were the biggest windows in a ship where some of the rooms below decks had none.

Captain Skrimshank was busy writing in a ledger marked 'LOG BOOK' as Mr Briggs knocked on the door and led Eddie and Lady Constance into the cabin. He was dressed as he was always dressed, in a beautifully clean and pressed uniform, which looked fresh on that morning.

Eddie had never actually seen Captain Skrimshank do much, except walk about the various decks, once in a while, with his hands clasped behind his back, whilst his men acknowledged him with a salute, a nod, a greeting of 'Cap'n', or all three. He certainly looked the part, though. Eddie could imagine him being a Royal Navy captain with a ship bristling with cannons, rather than the captain of a clipper – a merchant ship.

When Eddie had been confused with that other trunk all those years ago and first sent to sea, the sailing ship he'd been on had been entirely made of wood. Although, at first glance, the *Pompous Pig* also looked wooden, she – yup, ships were referred to as though they were women back then, something which only changed at Lloyds of London (the mighty ship insurers) in the year 2002, which sounds pretty recent to me – was what was called a 'composite'; planks of wood over an iron frame.

If you think it odd that Eddie and Lady Constance were travelling in a sailing ship – relying on the wind and currents – long after steamships had been invented, I should point out that a nifty sail-powered clipper could easily do 16 to 18 knots an hour (a 'knot' being a measure of distance, as well as something to do with string) whereas, back then, most big, bulky steamships could only do a mere 12 knots and needed to carry huge amounts of coal to burn.

'Mr Briggs tells me that you have a plan for enticing your errant great-aunt out of hiding,' said Captain Skrimshank rising from his seat and nodding his head in deference to Lady Constance, pausing for a brief second or two to admire his features in a small, circular looking-glass riveted to the wall. 'And that something shiny is in order.'

'The shinier the better, Captain,' said Eddie, still in his underwear because his dried clothes had mysteriously gone missing.

The captain unbuttoned the top of his tunic and pulled a gold chain from around his neck. On it was a large key. He handed it to Spartacus Briggs. 'If you would do the honours, Mr Briggs?' he said. While Mr Briggs took the key and proceeded to open the safe with it, Captain Skrimshank continued to talk. 'Are you aware what cargo it is that we're carrying to America on this particular voyage?' he asked.

'From what I was able to gather from your men, you have a cargo hold full of shoes,' said Eddie.

'Left shoes,' added Lady Constance.

'Exactly right,' said the captain. 'A recently mechanised shoe factory in Nottingham ran into serious problems with its machinery and could only produce shoes for the left foot, as opposed to matching pairs. This would have led to serious financial losses and even the loss of jobs had it not been for the brilliance of the owner's son, Young Mr Dunkle – as opposed to the owner himself, who was called "Old Mr Dunkle", that is. Mr Dunkle Junior was aware of the newly opened Ooops Hospital in Boston Massachusetts set up specifically for those who have lost limbs in accidents. He has secured the sole contract, no pun intended, for supplying shoes for one-legged patients whose remaining leg is of the left variety. The patients are delighted to be wearing the latest fashions. The hospital is delighted at the reasonable price they have agreed upon, and Dunkle Footwear of Nottingham are delighted that their future is safe.'

'How very . . .' Eddie wondered what the captain's anecdote had to do with the Even Madder Aunt Maud situation, unless some of these left shoes had very shiny buckles which were placed in the safe for safe-keeping. (Hence the word safe.) '. . . interesting,' he said.

'Interesting in that the shoes are not the only cargo,' said Captain Skrimshank with a dramatic air. Mr Briggs had opened the safe and pulled out a red leather box about the size of one that could hold a single cricket ball. He handed it to the captain with great care. 'There is also this,' said the captain, twisting a gold clasp and slowly opening the lid of the box, 'and it is worth more than this entire ship and all those shoes put together.'

Eddie actually gasped. There, nestling in the crushed red velvet lining of the box, was a dazzling jewel. It reminded Eddie of the bauble from the chandelier, but that had been cut crystal glass; this was obviously a real diamond, sparkling like fire, and, at the very centre, was a flaw – a dark blemish or naturally formed mark – in the almost perfect shape of a cartoon dog's bone.

'It's . . . It's beautiful,' said the stunned Lady Constance. 'Even more beautiful than I ever dreamed possible. Surely this must be the world famous Dog's Bone Diamond?'

The captain nodded proudly. 'So named because of the shape of the flaw at the very heart of it. It was recently purchased from its British owner by Dr Eli Bowser, the American dog-food tycoon, and we aboard the *Pompous Pig* have been given the honour and responsibility of transporting it.'

'Wow!' said Eddie, which wasn't an everyday Victorian expression but neatly summed up how he felt. 'But why no armed guards? And surely a steamship would have been more reliable?' He was a bright kid.

'As a precaution,' the captain explained. 'As a subterfuge, if you like. Two days after we set sail, it was announced in the British and American press that the dazzling Dog's Bone Diamond was being sent to America, with an armed escort, aboard the American steamship *Pine Cone*. There are, indeed, two detectives from the Pickleton Detective Agency now aboard the *Pine Cone* and they are, indeed, guarding a so-called diamond, but even they don't know that it is a fake. If there are any crooks out there, their attention will be centred on the wrong ship!'

Eddie immediately thought of the escaped

convict Swags aboard *this* ship. He knew that he must say something at once. He was about to speak, but his travelling companion got in first.

'Was your idea to use this as the shiny bait to lure out Master Edmund's great-aunt?' asked Lady Constance, her eyes still on the diamond and nothing else.

'Yes,' said the captain. 'Unless someone's flying overhead in a hot-air balloon, our secret is going to remain on board. We're still a good few days away from land.'

Once again Eddie opened his mouth to mention the possible dangers of Swags and, once again, Lady Constance managed to jump in first.

'Too dangerous, Captain,' she said. 'What if his great-aunt actually managed to get hold of it before we could stop her and threw it overboard?'

'But why should she do that, Lady Constance?' asked a puzzled Skrimshank.

'The clue is in the name Even *Madder* Aunt Maud, Captain,' Eddie reminded him. 'Now I must talk to you about the other paying passeng–'

He got no further because there was a terrible smashing of glass and the terrifying figure of an elderly woman, half-covered in seaweed, came crashing through the window of the captain's cabin, swinging on a thick rope, with a slightly battered-looking stuffed stoat under one arm.

Before anyone realised quite what was going on, she had landed on the floor, snatched the dazzling Dog's Bone Diamond from the stunned captain's hand and dashed out on to the wheel deck.

The others rushed out after Even Madder Aunt Maud just in time to see her trip and lose her grip on the Dog's Bone Diamond. It rolled across the wheel deck, like the peppermint from the detective inspector's ear, and over the edge and out of sight. For a moment, everyone watched in horror, frozen to the spot . . . then there was a sudden dash to look over the edge to the main deck below to see what had happened.

There had been no sound of diamond-hitting-wood. Just an eerie silence. Perhaps it had landed on a coil of rope or some burlap sacking? No. There was none directly below; just bare boards. And no sign of the diamond. That end of the deck appeared to be deserted.

Captain Skrimshank whimpered whilst Mr Briggs was already running down the wooden ladder joining the decks, two rungs at a time. Powder Monkey and Eddie, meanwhile, were helping Even Madder Aunt Maud to her feet. Fortunately, she seemed none the worse for wear for having lived rough, swung Tarzan-like through a window and fallen on the deck . . . but, at least it had subdued her. It was only later that it occurred to Eddie that Lady Constance was nowhere to be seen.

*

Despite a shipwide search, there was no sign of the missing diamond and the captain was beside himself – now there's a phrase that's impossible to act out in real life, without the aid of mirrors – with anguish. Considering Even Madder Aunt Maud had been a stowaway and entirely to blame for the gem's loss, Eddie thought the captain was being incredibly reasonable about the whole thing; simply confining her to her (well, to *Eddie's*) quarters and insisting that Eddie not leave her alone for one second.

The frustrating part was that Skrimshank wouldn't let Eddie get a word in edgeways concerning his suspicions about Swags . . . suspicions which now included the one that the Dog's Bone Diamond was probably in the escaped convict's hands!

Eddie concluded that Swags must have somehow got wind of the fact that the priceless diamond was on board the *Pompous Pig* and had become a paying passenger with a view to stealing it from the safe . . . until Even Madder Aunt Maud had – almost literally – let it drop into his lap. Eddie was as sure as he could be, without having actually witnessed it, that Swags had been lucky enough to have been on the main deck when the jewel had come falling towards it. It must have seemed like a gift from heaven!

Fully aware that Even Madder Aunt Maud (and Malcolm, of course) wouldn't have set foot on the ship – and so wouldn't have created an opportunity to steal the diamond – if he hadn't been on board in the first place, and the fact that the shiny-thing-as-bait idea had been his, Eddie felt responsible for the theft of the diamond. He wanted to put things right for Captain Skrimshank, even if it meant disobeying orders and leaving his great-aunt on her own.

Eddie felt somewhat guilty, but he decided the safest thing to do would be to tie up Even Madder Aunt Maud, to stop her wandering. He didn't want to tie her wrists and ankles – that would be most painful and undignified and not something any great-nephew should ever have to do to a great-aunt, mad or otherwise – so he waited until she dropped off to sleep (in his bed, as a matter of fact) and then wrapped a coil of rope around her *and* the bed, like an extra-tight blanket. Tiptoeing to his cabin door, he heard his aunt happily muttering something to do with 'prunes' in her sleep, blissfully unaware she was a prisoner.

Taking one last glance back at her as he gingerly turned the door handle, Eddie thought how cosy she and Malcolm looked, tucked up together like that. He stepped out of the cabin and into the night.

The *Pompous Pig* seemed very different bathed in silvery moonlight. Familiar objects seemed to take on different forms. The barrel to Eddie's left, for example, appeared to be moving.

'Whatcha up to?' asked the barrel.

If this had been a TV cartoon, Eddie would have jumped out of his skin, leaving it on the deck like a discarded pile of crumpled clothes.

'Who – ?' he blurted. Then, quickly regaining his senses, he added an urgent 'sssh!' He had recognised that this was no barrel, it was the boy Powder Monkey.

'I'm sure I's heard the cap'n tells you to stay with that dotty old lady of yours,' whispered the galley hand, with a wicked grin.

'Do I know you?' asked Eddie. 'Have we met before . . . somewhere on dry land, I mean? You do look very familiar.'

''Course we 'ave,' said Powder Monkey. 'The last time you saw me, I was hittin' some strange bloke with a cucumber.'

It all made sense in an instant. 'You're an orphan from St Horrid's Home for Grateful Orphans!' said Eddie, a little louder than he should have, what with all the excitement.

'That's right,' whispered the boy, 'an' you're the one what helped us all escape an' that. What's you up to this time?'

Eddie quickly told his new ally about Swags, and his belief that he must have the gem. 'With you to help me, that should make things a whole lot easier,' Eddie concluded.

'How's that?' asked Powder Monkey.

'If you could knock on his door and get him out of his cabin – making some excuse about Mr Briggs wanting to see him and then leading him on some wild goose chase around the ship – that should give me time to search it for the missing diamond.'

'But I don't have no goose,' said Powder Monkey.

'No what I meant was –'

'An' if I did, it'd be a tame goose, not a wild one –'

'No, I simply meant –'

'And what if Mr Swags didn't wanta chase it anyways?'

Eddie grabbed Powder Monkey by the shoulders. 'Forget the goose!' he hissed. 'I wish I'd never mentioned the goose . . . Could you tell Swags some lie about Mr Briggs needing to see him below decks, then get him well and truly lost down there?'

'Sure I can,' said Powder Monkey, giving Eddie a strange look. 'I don't need no goose for that.'

'I asked you to forget the goose,' Eddie

reminded him.

'What goose?' grinned Powder Monkey.

'Good,' said Eddie, grinning back. At last, they were getting somewhere. 'Excellent.'

Keeping to the shadows, they made their way towards the door of Swags's cabin. Hearing footsteps on the wooden decking, they hid behind a huge coil of rope and stood as still as they humanly could.

Eddie listened. The steps were 'clackerty' and close together, which suggested short strides in women's shoes and, apart from Even Madder Aunt Maud, the only woman on board was Lady Constance Bustle. But what was she doing up and about at this hour? Especially when she'd said goodnight to Eddie, several hours earlier, just before she'd said that she was 'retiring to bed'.

Perhaps she'd got up for a glass of water, or something, and looked into his cabin to find EMAM trussed up like a chicken, and that he – Eddie – was nowhere to be seen. He sincerely hoped that wasn't the case.

The person responsible for the footsteps walked past them in the dark and, sure enough, it was indeed Lady Constance. She had a grim, determined expression on her face. She headed purposefully towards the prow – the pointy bit at the front – of the ship. Eddie and Powder Monkey followed. There was someone waiting for her. When Eddie saw who it was, his heart sank (in much the same way that Gibbering Jane's had when she'd come out from under the stairs, back home, to find out what had made that nasty 'CRUNCH' in the hallway).

Lady Constance's secret late-night rendezvous was with none other than Swags himself.

Episode 11

Going Overboard

In which various characters pick themselves up, dust themselves down and start all over again

Fortunately for Mad Uncle Jack, he was none the worse for falling from Eddie's father's scaffolding rig because he landed on top of Dawkins – Awful End's gentleman's gentleman – thus cushioning the impact.

Fortunately for Dawkins, who had happened to be crossing the floor of the hallway at exactly the right/wrong moment, a free-falling MUJ wasn't too heavy a person to be hit with. Being so thin, he was more arms and legs and beak-like nose than anything else. Still, it's not very pleasant having anyone land on top of one unexpectedly, and poor old Dawkins ended up in bed for six weeks, as a result. (It would have been seven but Mr Dickens was getting desperate to have someone tie his ties for him.)

Because Dr Humple didn't want to move Dawkins too far from the scene of the accident, for fear of doing him more harm than good, and because it was agreed that Gibbering Jane should be the one to look after him, Dawkins's bed was brought downstairs.

The head end was stuck through the doorway to the cupboard under the stairs so that Jane could feed him, mop his brow, etc., whilst still being able to remain in familiar surroundings. The rest of the bed stuck out into the hallway. Sometimes Eddie's father would shout down with words of encouragement, flat on his back, from high above.

Mad Uncle Jack and Eddie's mother, Mrs Dickens, meanwhile, were on a steam vessel heading in the direction of America. Yup, you read that right. That's what that picture over there, at the beginning of this episode, is all about!

Unable to bear any more time apart from his beloved Maud than absolutely necessary, MUJ had decided to set off in hot pursuit of the *Pompous Pig*. He had chartered the 'steamglider' *Belch II* because of its speed.

Without going into too much boring detail, which would require a few diagrams and pages and pages of explanation (when there are less than twenty-four left to finish the entire story), suffice it to stay that what powered the engine of a *steam* vessel was, as you might possibly have guessed without a degree in mechanical engineering, steam and what created the steam was water heated to boiling point by burning coal.

The problem arose if you had to go any great distance. You needed an ENORMOUS amount of coal. You didn't need a big ship simply to carry the passengers, you needed it big to house the fuel to make it go anywhere in the first place!

Whilst people were up on deck sipping lovely drinkies and saying, ''Ain't it a beautiful morning?' gangs of men were down in the bowels of the ship stoking the boilers; not with unwanted tally sticks but with shovel after shovel of coal.

Fortunately, this was sort of solved when a new kind of steam engine, called a double-expansion engine, was invented. It made much more use out of the same amount of steam so (as the mathematically minded amongst you will have gathered) this meant more distance, or speed, for less coal.

The *Belch II* was designed and built by Tobias Belch, who later became *Sir* Tobias and is best remembered today for having invented one of the first watches to be worn on the wrist, rather than kept on a chain or in a pocket, though, unfortunately, it too was steam-powered and could cause nasty burns. His 'steamglider' had an even newer and more remarkable engine which he called the 'quadruple-expansion engine' or 'Sweet Nancy' (when he was whispering to it, to try to encourage it to go faster). This, he claimed, needed so little coal that the *Belch II* could be smaller and faster, and the 'steamglider' had quadruple propellers too which, apparently, was also a good thing. The fact that Sir Tobias – then plain *Mr* Belch – was a person way ahead of his time was borne out by the fact that he wore shorts instead of trousers and, not only that, they had a bright flowery pattern on them.

He was sporting a pair of such shorts as he steered the *Belch II* with one hand and consulted a navigational chart with the other. 'Of course, the *Pompous Pig* is dependent on the winds and we may miss her altogether but, with luck on our side, we could catch up with her any day now,' he told Mad Uncle Jack, who was leaning against a railing, dressed in a sailor suit similar to one he'd worn as a boy. Mrs Dickens was, in the meantime, stoking the small boiler. Both had lost count of the number of days they'd been at sea. Mrs Dickens found that she was a natural-born stoker and was enjoying every minute of it. On more than one occasion, Tobias Belch had told her to stop stoking because it'd be a waste of fuel. The quadruple-expansion engine – Nancy – was doing very nicely without it, thank you very much.

Thanks to the brilliance of his engineering and the skill of his sailing (or whatever it is you call handling a sea-going vessel without sails), Tobias Belch finally caught up with the *Pompous Pig*, despite its many days' head start. This also had something to do with the fact that the ship was at anchor. In other words it was 'parked' and not going anywhere.

Using a big whistle to attract attention, and some flag waving (called semaphore) to explain their intention, *Belch II* was soon alongside the *Pompous Pig* and Mad Uncle Jack and Mrs Dickens were soon scaling up the side of the clipper on the rope ladder, Eddie's mother relieved that she no longer needed crutches.

'Where's my darling Maud?' cried MUJ.

'Where's little Edmund?' asked his mother.

Mr Spartacus Briggs and a small cluster of sailors were waiting for them on deck. He stepped forward. 'I have grave news,' he said, not sure where to begin.

Lady Constance Bustle made her way to the front of the welcoming party, fluttered her eyelashes at Mr Briggs and whispered, 'Let me do it, Spartacus.' She then turned to the Dickenses. 'These are truly terrible times,' she said. 'I am sad to report that a number of people – passengers and crew – were washed overboard in the early hours of the morning two days ago . . .'

'My love-cheese?' gasped Mad Uncle Jack.

'Your lady wife is fine, sir,' Mr Briggs reassured him, placing a reassuring hand upon his shoulder. 'She is currently resting with her stuffed stoat in Master Edmund's cabin, tied firmly to her bed.'

'Unbounded joy,' Mad Uncle Jack pronounced.

'And Edmund?' asked Mrs Dickens. 'My Edmund?'

'He was not so lucky, Mrs D,' said Lady Constance, who was used to imparting bad news to relatives because she did it so often. 'I'm afraid he was washed overboard . . .'

'Deep sorrow,' interjected Mad Uncle Jack.

Mrs Dickens simply wailed.

'Along with our very own Captain Skrimshank, a galley hand and another paying passenger . . .' added Mr Briggs, eager to emphasise that the shipping company as well as the Dickenses were suffering a loss. It somehow seemed less careless that way. 'We've been circling around looking for them for days,' he went on. 'I'm afraid there's no sign of them.'

Mrs Dickens sobbed some more. Well, mothers can be like that, can't they?

'The wave came out of nowhere,' said Lady Bustle. 'It was a calm sea on a moonlit night. I witnessed the whole thing with my own eyes. I was out on deck taking a midnight stroll when I saw the galley hand –'

'His name was Powder Monkey and he was on night watch,' Mr Briggs interrupted. 'He was a good lad . . . Would have made a fine sailor one day.'

'I saw the galley hand in conversation with young Master Dickens, the captain and the one other paying passenger called Mr Smith,' Lady Constance explained. She crouched down next to Mrs Dickens who had crumpled to the deck, and put a comforting arm around her. 'A jewel had gone missing and one of them had found it. They were excited and happy and I could see it in the captain's hand.' Her tone changed. 'A moment later, a huge wave came out of nowhere, washing them overboard . . . It was so fast and so unexpected that they didn't have a chance to let out so much as a cry. I dashed across the soaking deck to raise the alarm but slipped and knocked myself unconscious.' She touched a small bruise on her forehead. 'I could do nothing until I came to my senses many hours later.'

There was silence. Even those who'd heard tell of the events before were still horrified by them. That two boys and two men should be lost in that fleeting moment, not forgetting one of the most valuable and famous jewels in the world . . .

'LIAR!' said a loud voice behind them.

Members of the not-so-welcoming welcome committee that had clustered around Mad Uncle Jack and Mrs Dickens parted to reveal – yes, you guessed it (or, at least, you cheated and looked at the picture) – a bedraggled Eddie Dickens climbing aboard the ship.

'You're alive!' his mother squealed with delight and, with one of the few signs of affection he was ever to receive from her, she threw her arms around him and squeezed him tight. 'You smell of turtles!' she added.

Eddie's mother never ceased to amaze him. How did she know what turtles smelt like? But she was right. He'd ridden on the back of a turtle through the waves to get back to the ship. He'd had to help with the steering, of course, because he had a specific destination and couldn't talk Turtlese (or whatever turtles speak; I've never even heard one make a noise) but it was very friendly and seemed to thoroughly enjoy the whole experience.

'Lady Constance is a liar and, if her plan had worked, would be a murderer, too!' shouted Eddie. 'Don't worry, Mr Briggs. The captain and the others are alive and well and ready for rescue!'

'The boy is clearly deranged!' said Lady Constance. 'Loopy! Ga-ga! The whole dreadful experience has turned his mind!'

'I think I might be able to prove it,' said Eddie, walking towards her across the deck, leaving a trail of seawater behind him. Despite her being much taller than him, and him not carrying any type of weapon, she backed away. She knew what he was going to say next.

'How?' asked Mr Briggs uncertainly. He looked from the supposedly drowned boy to the titled lady.

'She said that the Dog's Bone Diamond was washed overboard, but I know where she's hidden it! She was bragging about it . . . taunting us with it . . .' He paused. 'Before she forced us into the leaking rowing boat.'

The crowd – made up of many more sailors who'd come to see what all the fuss was about – gasped (which is nice because it adds to the drama; even if they hadn't gasped, I might have *said* they did, just to make it sound better . . . but they did, anyway, so I don't have to).

'Potty, I tell you,' cried Lady Bustle. 'The boy's gone potty.'

Mr Briggs looked at her sadly. 'Then you won't mind if he shows us where he thinks it is,' said Mr Briggs.

The still-dripping Eddie led the way to his cabin and threw open the door. Even Madder Aunt Maud was still lashed to the bed, as Eddie had left her two nights previously.

'About time too!' said his great-aunt as everyone piled into the cabin. 'I am due to marry the Archbishop of Canterbury at midday and must have my moustache curled.'

'My dreamboat!' said Mad Uncle Jack, throwing

his arms around her tightly trussed body.

'Remove this man!' shouted Mad Aunt Maud. 'Have him shot!'

But Eddie wasn't listening. He pulled Malcolm the stuffed stoat out from beside her and pointed to some bright red stitching.

'Unpick that!' he said.

Lady Constance made a dash for the cabin door, only to find it barred by 'Jolly' Roger. 'I think you 'ad better be waitin' in 'ere, m'lady, until Mr Briggs says otherwise,' he said.

Briggs produced a knife from his pocket and cut through the stitching with one swipe of the blade.

Mad Aunt Maud's eyes widened in horror. 'Murderer!' she cried.

'Don't worry,' Eddie reassured her, feeling inside the stuffed stoat and pulling out the Dog's Bone Diamond with a triumphant flourish. 'A bit of fresh stuffing and Malcolm will be as right as rain!'

'How on Earth did he swallow that?' cried Even Madder Aunt Maud. 'Silly, silly boy!'

Mr Briggs took the fabulous jewel and held it up in front of Lady Constance's face. 'How do you explain this?' he asked.

'I – er – Anyone could have put it there,' she protested.

'But you said that you saw it being washed overboard,' Mr Briggs reminded her.

'I saw *him* go overboard, too,' said Lady Constance, 'and he's back.'

'The stitching,' said Eddie. 'Look at the stitching.'

'That doesn't tell you anything,' said Lady Constance. 'They looked like perfectly normal stitches to me, cleverly concealed if one didn't know where to look . . . which *you* somehow, and somewhat suspiciously, did, Master Edmund!'

'Cleverly concealed?' said a puzzled Mr Briggs and there were a few murmurs from the assembled company.

'Malcolm ate something that didn't agree with him and Eddie and that nice man operated to remove it,' Even Madder Aunt Maud was telling Mad Uncle Jack, who was now busy untying her. Both seemed blissfully unaware of the drama unfolding around them.

Eddie held up a piece of cut thread from the stitching. 'It's bright red and doesn't match Malcolm's fur in the slightest,' said Eddie. 'But, when we first met, Lady Constance told me that she has Dalton's Disease, which means that she has a kind of colour blindness . . .'

'And mistakenly thought that the stitching blended in with the ferret's fur,' said Mr Briggs.

139

He then added an 'ouch' because Even Madder Aunt Maud had just hit him over the head with Malcolm.

'He's a stoat,' she told him.

Episode 12

Back and Forth

In which we go backwards and forwards
in order to try to make sense of it all

When matters were explained to Tobias Belch, he quickly agreed to take his 'steamglider' to the tiny island – more of a large sandy bump in the ocean than anything else – where Eddie had informed them the others were awaiting rescue. Obviously, Eddie had to accompany him for it was only he who (he hoped) knew the way. Mr Briggs insisted on coming too because he felt it his duty to be on the rescue mission that saved his captain. Jolly was put in charge of the *Pompous Pig*, with strict instructions that Even Madder Aunt Maud wasn't allowed to touch anything, and that Lady Constance must remain locked in her cabin, with a guard on each door.

As *Belch II* steamed off, Eddie now had a chance to tell Mr Briggs what had led to his disappearance, along with the captain, the galley hand and the third paying passenger . . .

. . . On that fateful moonlit night, two nights previously, Eddie couldn't believe his eyes when he saw Lady Constance deep in conversation with Swags.

'They know each other!' he whispered to Powder Monkey, who was crouching next to him in the shadow of a huge barrel – which really was a barrel this time – marked 'SHIP'S BISCUITS'.

'I don't fink vey do, ya know,' Powder Monkey whispered back. 'She appears to be makin' introductions.'

It was true. Creeping as near as he dare, Eddie could hear Lady Constance saying: '. . . and, though I don't know your real name, I know that you're the escaped convict they call Swags.'

'Am I supposed to be impressed by that?' asked Swags, with a voice that made his flesh creep. 'The boy told you. That's all.'

'But no one has told the captain. *Yet*,' said Lady

Constance. Her meaning was very clear.

Eddie couldn't hear what Swags said next but he certainly didn't look the happiest person on the ship.

'Now, of course, if you and I were to share the profits from a little something you have . . .' Lady Constance paused.

'I don't have anything you want, lady,' said Swags and he made the word 'lady' sound far from ladylike, which was fair enough when you think about it. Eddie's official travelling companion was turning out to be on the nasty side of not-so-nice, and (as those of you reading these pages in order will already know) her worst was yet to come.

'You have *exactly* what I want, Mr Swags, but I'm prepared to share it,' she went on. 'I'm willing to bet my life that you have the Dog's Bone Diamond somewhere about your person' (which means 'somewhere on you'). 'Agree to split the profits when you have it cut down into smaller gems and sold, and your secret remains just that: a secret.'

Swags turned and faced out to sea and, once again, Eddie couldn't hear what he was saying, but there was absolutely no doubt what he saw. Lady Constance slipped her hand deep into an outer pocket of the convict's tatty coat and, with the nimble fingers of an experienced pickpocket, pulled out the diamond!

When Swags realised what had happened, he raised his arm as if to hit her and she grabbed his wrist. 'If you think I came to this meeting armed with nothing more than a hat pin, you've seriously underestimated me!' she hissed.

Eddie decided that it was time to report what he'd found to the captain. Leaving Powder Monkey to keep an eye on Swags and Bustle, Eddie found the captain in his cabin. Despite the hour, he was still seated at his chart-covered table and still fully dressed in his splendid uniform. What was slightly less impressive was that he was asleep, his head resting, face down, in a plate of cold shepherd's pie. (And, no, like the badger back on page 5, I'm afraid I can't tell you what the poor shepherd died of.)

144

When Eddie woke Skrimshank and told him about the two villains and the Dog's Bone Diamond, the captain was out of his chair and out of the cabin before Eddie had time to think.

'Shouldn't we get reinforcements?' he asked the captain, trying to keep up.

'I can handle this pair!' he reassured Eddie with confidence.

The confidence was, of course, completely unfounded. By the time Eddie and Captain Skrimshank reached Lady Constance and Swags, the scheming twosome – ooo, isn't that a nice phrase? – had already discovered Powder Monkey lurking near by; without Eddie there to hold him back, the ex-St Horrid's Home orphan had become overconfident and less cautious. Swags had grabbed the boy so had a ready-made hostage the moment Eddie and the captain arrived on the scene.

'Put that boy down!' the captain shouted.

Swags, who was holding Powder Monkey by the scruff of the neck, now lifted the boy over the edge of the ship. 'Any more shouting and the boy goes in the water,' he warned.

'I believe you have in your possession something which belongs to Dr Eli Bowser,' said Skrimshank (his voice much lower now). 'Put the boy down and return the jewel and I will go easy on you.'

145

Lady Constance laughed. 'I have a better idea,' she said. And they soon found out what it was. They were to be cast adrift in the tiny rowing boat.

Eddie was the first one forced down the side of the *Pompous Pig* into the boat. Next went the captain. He didn't resist (not only because Swags still had Powder Monkey in his vice-like grip but also because he felt it his duty to stay with a fare-paying passenger in distress). Swags came down next, with the struggling galley hand tucked under his arm. Now they were in the boat, Swags tied Eddie's, Skrimshank's and, finally, Powder Monkey's hands behind their backs, cutting the pieces of rope to length with an evil-looking knife – can knives look evil? – that conveniently glinted in the moonlight or glinted in the convenient moonlight. (Moonlight isn't really moonlight, by the way, it's simply sunlight reflected off the moon. Think about it. The moon isn't on fire like the sun, and doesn't have a great big battery inside it, so where did you think the light was coming from?)

Now where were we? Yup, that's it: Eddie, Skrimshank and Powder Monkey bound and, whilst I was doing the 'is-moonlight-moonlight?' bit, gagged so that they couldn't cry for help once cast adrift. That done, Swags began to climb back up the side of the *Pompous Pig*. A surprise greeted him at the top of the ladder. Lady Constance gave him a swift bash over the head with the Dog's Bone Diamond . . . and diamond is the hardest substance known to humankind.

The escaped convict fell into the sea with a SPLASH loud enough to attract any sailor on nightwatch, the only trouble being that Powder Monkey was the one on watch and there wasn't much he could do about it!

Lady Constance leant over the side of the ship and spoke to her captives. 'I'm so sorry it had to end this way, gentlemen,' she said and, although her tone did sound ever-so-slightly apologetic, none of them believed, for one moment, that she was sorry.

'You will be pleased to know, Master Edmund, that I have thought of the ideal place to hide the diamond. It's a place no one will ever think of looking and, once your dear sweet batty great-aunt is untied, no one will be able to get near. I shall stitch it up in that stuffed ferret of hers!'

'Oah!' cried Eddie, which is what it sounds like if you try to say 'Stoat!' through a gag when tied up in a rowing boat set adrift in the Atlantic Ocean . . . or at least it did in Eddie's case.

As it turned out, Lady Constance's cruellest act was what saved them all that night. Gagged, Eddie and his companions in the rowing boat couldn't shout to attract attention or speak to each other. Bound, they couldn't take out the gags or untie each other, let alone swim. But Swags was neither bound nor gagged.

After what seemed like ages, the tiny rowing boat had drifted almost out of sight of the *Pompous Pig* and the three had given up trying to make each other understood through their gags. What was worse was that the boat appeared to have sprung a leak. Perhaps it had always been there, but now the bottom of the boat was beginning to fill with sea water, or should that be ocean water? I doubt it makes much difference when you're drowning.

Then Swags broke through the surface of the water right beside them and hauled himself aboard. Without so much as a word, he untied the captain

148

and then collapsed, exhausted from his swim, in what little space there was. Skrimshank quickly untied Eddie who, in turn, untied Powder Monkey.

Eddie eyed the half-sleeping Swags, a cut from the Dog's Bone Diamond sending a trickle of blood down his forehead. 'He probably saved our lives!' said Eddie.

'What little good it'll do him,' said the captain. 'He put us in this predicament in the first instance,' which means 'he got us into this mess'.

'It's probably too late to save us now anyways,' said a sad and dejected Powder Monkey, who was still feeling guilty for getting himself caught and being the hostage that made the others do as they were told.

But, as we of the all's-well-that-ends-well persuasion already know, it wasn't too late. By luck or fate or a fluke of geography, when the four had to abandon the boat – then sinking – and make a swim for it, a tiny island (aka sandy hummock *not* hammock) haven had come into view within swimming distance . . . and they all made it there.

Within a matter of hours, Captain Skrimshank's uniform had dried and, with a little help from Powder Monkey, looked as good as new. Swags had lost his knife in the fall from the *Pompous Pig*, and his dignity, too. He had saved the others

149

because he'd needed them as much as they'd needed him now that he'd been double-crossed by Lady C. They were all alone, apart from a very friendly family of giant sea turtles who had obviously never met these funny-looking shell-less animals called 'humans' that had crawled out of the sea before.

'And it was the largest turtle that finally brought me all the way back to the *Pompous Pig*,' Eddie told Mr Briggs, coming to the end of his tale, just as the first mate spotted the others on the island in the distance, and Tobias Belch steered *Belch II* in their direction. Once again, Eddie had saved the day!

So that, dear reader, just about wraps up the third and final book in the Eddie Dickens Trilogy. As I did at the end of *Awful End* and *Dreadful Acts*, though, I should, of course, tie up a few loose ends before I say 'goodbye'.

The question most of you will, no doubt, write and ask me about if I don't answer it here is whether Eddie finally got to America, the Eastern Seaboard and the offices of the *Terrible Times*? The answer is simple: no. Sad to say, he abandoned all attempts to set foot on American soil this time. He went back to England with his mother, Mad Uncle Jack, Even Madder Aunt Maud, a newly repaired Malcolm, and (the then plain 'Mr') Tobias Belch aboard *Belch II*.

As it turned out, there had indeed been what the editor called 'a few glitches' at the *Terrible Times* offices, the worst of which was the editor's wife falling into the printing presses. This particular glitch not only caused a loss of three editions whilst the presses were repaired and the pearls from her broken necklace recovered, but it also meant that Mrs Brockenfeld (the editor of the *Terrible Times* being *Mr* Brockenfeld) was never quite the same shape again. On meeting her for the first time, people found it hard to tell whether she was greeting them frontways or sideways on. She had a 'permanent profile' look about her, something which, in the following century, an artist called Pablo Picasso painted his women to look like and made a small fortune in so doing.

Mr Brockenfeld had been so embarrassed by the whole accident incident that he'd missed sending his regular report to the Dickenses in England because he hadn't known what to say. Had he known Eddie's relatives better, he needn't have worried. If Even Madder Aunt Maud had worked for the newspaper, she'd have probably clambered into the presses deliberately and on numerous occasions!

And what of the not-so-ladylike Lady Constance Bustle and Swags? They were taken to America on board the *Pompous Pig* but not allowed to set foot ashore. Once the cargo of left shoes was unloaded and the Dog's Bone Diamond delivered, they were brought back to England and ended up on trial. Swags, whose real name turned out to be Albert Grubb, was eventually sent back to Australia for thirty years' more hard labour and ended his days breaking rocks. Lady Constance ended up marrying the trial judge who died soon after. Apparently he and Lady Constance had been practising an amateur knife-throwing routine when she'd slipped on a bar of soap and stabbed him through the heart.

The Dog's Bone Diamond was duly handed over to Dr Eli Bowser 'the dog-food baron' who, on learning of a certain Eddie Dickens's part in saving it from harm, sent the boy an envelope stuffed with one thousand dollar bills, by way of a 'thank you'. Unfortunately for Eddie, the envelope somehow found its way to Even Madder Aunt Maud instead of him. She tore the money into tiny strips and wallpapered the inside of Marjorie with it. The truth be told, it certainly looked better than the ceiling of Awful End once Mr Dickens had finished painting it.

But, do you know what? Despite this and having some of the most embarrassing relatives in the history of humankind, on returning from his latest adventure, Eddie Dickens had to admit that there was no place like home . . . even when that home was Awful End.

Goodbye.

THE END
of the Eddie Dickens Trilogy

Awful End
Book One of the Eddie Dickens Trilogy

ISBN: 0 571 20354 X
£4.99 (Paperback)

When both of Eddie Dickens's parents catch a disease that makes them turn yellow, go a bit crinkly round the edges and smell of hot water bottles, it's agreed he should go and stay with relatives at their house Awful End. Unfortunately for Eddie, those relatives are Mad Uncle Jack and Even Madder Aunt Maud and they definitely live up to their names. This is the first book in the wildly successful Eddie Dickens Trilogy, set in a 19th-century world of blotchy skin, runaway orphans . . . and a stuffed stoat called Malcolm. One sitting and you'll be hooked.

Praise for *Awful End*

'[A] scrumptious cross between Dickens and Monty Python . . . Brilliant.'
Guardian

'In this surreal world, language is never what it appears . . . It's daft but entirely engaging.'
Independent

'. . . sophisticated. . . extremely silly . . . wonderful . . . ridiculing literary conventions and turning nonsense into a fine art.'
Sunday Telegraph

'It would be a sad spirit that didn't find this book hilarious.'
Financial Times

www.philipardagh.com

Dreadful Acts

Book Two of the Eddie Dickens Trilogy

ISBN: 0 571 20947 5

£4.99 (Paperback)

In this sequel to *Awful End*, our hero Eddie Dickens narrowly avoids an explosion, being hit by a hot-air balloon and being arrested, only to find himself falling head-over heels for a girl, called Daniella, with a face like a camel's. Unfortunately for Eddie, he also falls into the hands of a murderous gang of escaped convicts who have 'one little job for him to do'. All the old favourite characters are here, along with a whole batch of crazy new ones!

Praise for *Dreadful Acts*

'One of my favourite comic characters is back . . . Ardagh skilfully continues the comic drama of his first Eddie Dickens story . . . and the result is equally delicious, and ridiculous.'
The Bookseller

'Be warned, *Dreadful Acts* made me laugh so much I had hiccups.'
Vivian French, author & reviewer

'[Readers] who enjoyed the barkingly mad world of *Awful End* . . . will not be disappointed!'
Times Educational Supplement

www.philipardagh.com

Unlikely Exploits Book 1
The Fall of Fergal

ISBN: 0 571 21069 4
£7.99 (Hardback)

ISBN: 0 571 21521 1
£4.99 (Paperback)

This first book in a NEW series is set in an unidentified country suffering from an unexpected outbreak of holes, where the flame-haired McNally children find themselves in The Dell hotel surrounded by a strange assortment of ridiculous characters, ranging from Charlie 'Twinkle-Toes' Tweedy, the house detective, to Mr Peach, a ventriloquist with a conveniently large moustache. With young Fergal falling to his death on page one, the only way for the McNallys is up . . .

Praise for *The Fall of Fergal*

'A wacky, playful, entertaining read . . . My squeamish ten-year-old took all in her stride and pronounced it terrific!'
Irish Times

'Ardagh's writing is completely off the wall and steeped in black humour. Destined to win hearts and minds of eager readers.'
The Scotsman

'An accomplished and entertaining comedy rather than a tragedy . . . lots of fun.'
Independent

'Ardagh has a growing following among young readers who enjoy fantastical stories driven by inventive illogicality and peopled with over-the-top characters.'
Sunday Times

www.philipardagh.com

LOOK OUT FOR:

Unlikely Exploits Book 2
Heir of Mystery

ISBN: 0 571 21094 5
£7.99 (Hardback)

In this second unlikely exploit, full of surprising twists and turns, the remaining McNally children – Jackie, Le Fay and the twins Josh and Albie – are mysteriously drawn to Fishbone Forest and the forgotten crumbling mansion, which lies at its heart. Here they meet the terrifying teddy-bear clutching Mr Maggs who is planning to make sweeping changes to the world . . . which is all rather unlikely, isn't it? Packed with humour, excitement and sadness, this is another sure-fire winner.

AND COMING SOON:

Unlikely Exploits Book 3
The Rise of the House of McNally

ISBN: 0 571 21707 9
£7.99 (Hardback)

What's it all about? You'll just have to wait and see. One thing you CAN be sure of, though, is lots of laughs and lots of very silly goings-on! After all, it's an unlikely exploit and by Philip Ardagh!

www.philipardagh.com

The world of Philip Ardagh is only a click away. Log on for lots of facts, fun and figures:

www.philipardagh.com

You will find many hilarious things plus the following:

☞ Strange (and normal) information about the author

☞ More details about the hilarious characters featured in the Philip Ardagh books

☞ Pictures and photographs to download

☞ Details of future Philip Ardagh books and events

☞ How to write to the author

www.philipardagh.com

The Philip Ardagh Club

COLLECT some fantastic **Philip Ardagh** merchandise.

WHAT YOU HAVE TO DO:
You'll find tokens to collect in all Philip Ardagh's fiction books published after 08/10/02. There are 2 tokens in each hardback and 1 token in each paperback. Cut them out and send them to us complete with the form (below) and you'll get these great gifts:

2 tokens = a sheet of groovy character stickers
4 tokens = an Ardagh pen
6 tokens = an Ardagh rucksack

Please send with your collected tokens and the name & address form to:
Philip Ardagh promotion, Faber and Faber Ltd, 3 Queen Square, London, WC1N 3AU.

1. This offer can not be used in conjunction with any other offer and is non transferable. 2. No cash alternative is offered. 3. If under 18 please get permission and help from a parent or guardian to enter. 4. Please allow for at least 28 days delivery. 5. No responsibility can be taken for items lost in the post. 6. This offer will close on 31/12/04. 7. Offer open to readers in the UK and Ireland ONLY.

Name: ....
Address: ....
....
....
Town: ....
Postcode: ....
Age & Date of Birth: ....
Girl or boy: ....

Philip Ardagh Club
token